A
Second Call
To Serve

James J. Stewart

1.
The First Time

I screamed into my pillow again. It oozed with grief. I knew that time would lessen the pain, but my sorrow could not fill the hole in my heart. I will never forget. I can't. The pain may eventually fade, but the memories will not.

Before I get at the heart of my story, first you must have some background. My name is Frank Frazee. I'm a twelfth-generation pastor. My father and the fathers of ten generations before him were Anglican pastors. In my generation, I'm the oldest of ten, with five brothers and four sisters. My Dad was so proud when he baptized me! On the Saturday night before my baptismal immersion, some of the church's men formed a bucket brigade and filled the baptismal tank underneath the little church's chancel floor.

Being baptized on that January Sunday morning in Pittsburgh, Pennsylvania was truly memorable. There was a hard freeze Saturday night, and getting into the baptistery, Dad and I stepped through a half-inch of ice.

He did not seem to notice and spoke with his big bass voice. "This morning I have the great joy and privilege of baptizing my oldest son, Frank." Then and now, I'm tall, with plenty of meat on my bones, but I clenched my jaw as I tried to keep my teeth from chattering as I looked up at him. He continued. "Baptism means participation in Christ's death, burial, and resurrection...." He preached for over thirty minutes before he immersed me. I was numb, or so it seemed, for the rest of the day!

Nine years later, when I was eighteen, my Dad presided at my first marriage. As the Apostle Paul said, "If I speak in the tongues of men and of angels, but have not love, I am a noisy gong or a clanging cymbal." Elyse Johansson was my first love and my best friend since childhood. Growing up, we did everything together. I was a couple of inches over six feet, and she was five-five. On our wedding day, she wore the highest heels she could handle. As we said our vows, her glacial-blue eyes seemed to come to about my chin. Both of us were confident, as though we had been planning this day for many years. In a sense, that was true.

After the wedding, our marriage union was perfect except for her diabetes, which we had long before learned to take in stride. We honeymooned in Alaska, staying two weeks in a cabin at the foot of the mountain the natives have always called Denali. We made many still images and videos, and during those two weeks, the rest of the world was forgotten. We did not miss the daily newscasts, the continuing war in Viet Nam, or the civil unrest in the lower forty-eight. Right after our honeymoon, Elyse and I entered Pepperdine University, which is spread across the hills of Malibu in Southern California. Elyse wanted to take some courses in sociology, and I wanted to follow in my Dad's footsteps and get some kind of religion degree.

We loved the picturesque campus, and we enjoyed getting the exercise of trudging up and down the steep hills. Our first son, Mark, was born while I was taking summer classes at the end of our initial academic year there. Elyse dropped out of school to take care of Mark. Somehow, I managed to secure a position at Hughes Research Laboratories, just east of the campus on Malibu Canyon Road. I worked nights there as custodian. Elyse tutored a few young adults who wanted to pass their "GED." By the time I completed my degree and was ordained, Elyse and I were raising three children.

Elyse was infinitely patient with them, listening to them and talking with them. I read to them each evening, and I discussed whatever they wanted to talk about. Elyse and I both knew that these earliest years of their lives were crucially important, and we were mindful of preparing them for what they would face in school.

After graduation, my search for a pastoral position did not take long. My Dad tried to help with the search, but he was unsuccessful. Dad and I talked about it by phone every day or two. Matt Granger, a friend who graduated the previous year, recommended me to relatives of his in Kansas. After three telephone interviews, Elyse and I packed our car and headed east. Mom and Dad were supportive, but I knew that he was disappointed that I was not going on to a seminary and lead an Anglican church.

I began to serve a little community church at the edge of Kansas City, Missouri. As the pastor of a church started only three years earlier, I'm sure I appeared more confident than I actually was. Elyse put on a brave front as well for the sake of the children. Throughout all our years there, Elyse and I loved those folks, and they loved us. At first, during the week we watched the news every day as the Viet Nam war broke our hearts. Two sons and a daughter of families in our little church were over there already as we began our ministry there.

On our first Sunday there, there were forty-seven people in attendance. That initial Sunday, I called the congregation to worship with two verses from the 37th Psalm.

> Trust in the LORD, and do good; dwell in the land
> and befriend faithfulness. Delight yourself in the
> LORD, and he will give you the desires of your heart.
> [NIV]

At the end of the service, Elyse stood beside me as we greeted people because, while my memory for faces is fine, I don't remember names. Elyse remembered names easily, once she met anyone. Our little church grew. I enjoyed being called 'Pastor Frank.' Because of Elyse's dignity and poise, even when our children were giving her fits, the ladies at the church began calling her 'Lady Elyse.' She had mixed feelings about it, but the moniker stuck.

Time seemed to pass so quickly! Our seventh year, we took the summer off as a sabbatical leave, and we visited thriving churches and interviewed their pastors. On our tenth anniversary with the church, we had nine hundred seventy on our church rolls. The Elders repeatedly told me that we were growing because of my solidly biblical preaching. That summer, we broke ground for a new sanctuary that seated fifteen hundred comfortably. Less than five years after that, we began having two worship services in that new sanctuary. The old worship area was converted into a youth and children's facility.

By the time we reached our twentieth anniversary, we had passed two thousand a year earlier, and we hired a new Christian Education director named Debra Sue. She had just graduated from Brite Divinity School at Texas Christian University. Elyse immediately knew that Debra Sue was both brilliant and incredibly naïve. For Elyse, that brought out all of her mothering instincts.

My beloved wife urged me to help her make Debra Sue our personal project, so we did. The three of us became very close. We frequently ate dinner together, and after eating we would talk about church issues into the night. Sometimes Debra Sue would sleep on our sofa rather than go home after midnight.

Under Debra Sue's leadership, our Christian Education Department began to blossom. While Elyse and Debra Sue worked to get as many women involved beyond Sundays as possible, I worked with the men. We worked to strengthen families, with husbands and wives working as partners, building up one another in Christ's holiness.

With Elyse's experience and wisdom coupled with Debra Sue's energy and drive, they made many mother-daughter programs prosper. I followed suit with the men. I enlisted a few fathers to help me put on father-son events. The church sponsored periodic father-daughter group date nights, and also mother-son group date nights.

Each parent in their own way worked to define and live out their roles in their families. I preached one simple imperative regarding Christian marriage. When following Jesus and trying to be like Him, the husband and wife must encourage one another in that effort, working to build one another up in Christ's holiness. For the younger children, Elyse carefully trained the teachers. Debra Sue also developed some special programs for both tweens and teens. I baptized more tweens between nine and twelve than any other age group. Unfortunately, Elyse's diabetes began to get the better of her, despite Elyse's great care with her diet, insulin, and other medical issues. The first time Elyse had to spend overnight in the hospital, she recovered quickly, and just as soon, she resumed her roles as wife and mother. As time went on however, she spent longer in the hospital stays each time and recovered less rapidly.

The prayer circles began lifting up Elyse every day. She continued to read her Bible faithfully with me each day when we awakened. Her eyes did not start to bother her at first, and I prayed for her constantly. I also prayed with her whenever I was in her hospital room. Elyse and I celebrated our twenty-fifth "silver" anniversary at the hospital. Despite our doctor's best efforts and ours, her kidneys began to fail her, and her legs got so swollen she had difficulty walking.

On Easter Sunday evening in April, when my Family Ministries associate was preaching, Debra Sue and I went to the hospital to worship with Elyse. After Debra Sue and I sang a couple of praise songs, each of us read from the Bible and talked about why we picked that particular passage.

After we worshiped, Elyse was upbeat, though her voice was very weak. "I'm going to be going home soon."

Debra Sue smiled. "Really? What does the doctor say?"

Elyse shook her head. "I'm not talking about our home in Kansas City. I'm talking about my home in heaven."

I had seen this coming for about two weeks when we were praying together. "Don't you think you'll spring back again this time?"

"No, Frank, I know I won't. That's why I wanted the two people I love the most here to worship with me this evening."

I glanced at Debra Sue. There was a tear running down her cheek, and she reached for Elyse's hand. "I'm not ready for you to go home yet, Elyse."

Elyse gave her a weak smile. "I know, love, but you know as well as I do that all that God does, God does well. It's time." She paused. "You love my Frank, don't you?"

Debra Sue was understandably startled. "Why... why, yes, ... I suppose I do. Except for Jesus, Frank's the best friend I've ever had." She looked at me.

Elyse nodded. "I know. Frank?"

I had a knot in my stomach. "Yes, my love?"

"You love Debra Sue, don't you?"

I nodded. "She's like a precious daughter to me."

Elyse smiled again slightly. "When I return to heaven, I don't want either of you to be alone, and I think you will need each other when I'm gone."

"Elyse...." I began.

"Shush, Frank. After this body of flesh is in the ground, I want the two of you to wait maybe six months or so, and then I want you to get married."

Debra Sue's eyes got wide. "You don't mean this!"

"Yes, I do, Debra Sue. Do you remember Dr. John Wells, the man who founded the medical center over on the west side, and who retired last year?"

Debra Sue nodded. "John and Nancy had that big house on Lincoln Place, and they had a pet cheetah."

"Right. They intended to live in a condo in San Francisco, but they couldn't because of Sheila, the cheetah. They've built a big home in the Oakland Hills on a large parcel of land overlooking the bay. They've been wanting Frank and I to visit them. I think you should go with Frank to San Francisco for your honeymoon."

Debra Sue stared at her, dumbfounded and speechless. "You're serious, aren't you!"

"Absolutely, Debra Sue." She paused. "Frank, you're a truly Christ-centered man. You shun passivity, you accept responsibility, you lead courageously, and you look to the same greater reward that I will be going to shortly. Even if Debra Sue doesn't marry you, I want you to take responsibility for her as best you can. Will you?"

Elyse and I looked into each other's eyes as we had countless times before, then back to my beloved wife and partner. I could see the woman God knew before he formed Elyse in her late mother's womb. I nodded. "Okay." I swallowed and looked at Debra Sue. "Let's talk about this later."

Tears were running down her cheeks. "Okay."

That night, my Elyse slipped into a coma. Over the next six days, she went in and out, but finally she went home.

The church was filled beyond its capacity for the memorial service, and everyone on the staff had a part. Debra Sue and I went out to California and buried Elyse in a small, private service beside Elyse's parents at Rose Hills. That night was the first of many when I screamed into my pillow and oozed with grief before dropping off to sleep.

+ + +

Debra Sue stayed in California for a week, visiting with friends from her alma maters, Lakewood High School and Cal-State Long Beach. I did not preach the Sunday following Elyse's burial. I took a vacation Sunday and attended a church pastored by a friend from college days. The second Sunday after we buried Elyse, I was back in the pulpit, and Debra Sue returned and resumed supervision of the Church School and the children's and teen's evening programs.

After the evening service, Debra Sue and I met at 'A Little Barbeque Joint' in Independence, Missouri. As we ate rib dinners with hot potato salads, we talked. Through most of our meal, we talked about things we had done since the memorial service. In California, Debra Sue took in a movie premier in Hollywood with three of her friends from high school. I told her about how different the worship service was where I had attended there in Kansas City the previous Sunday.

After our waiter left our desserts in front of us, I looked at Debra Sue without lifting my fork. "For the last two weeks, I think I've thought every day about what Elyse asked us to do the Sunday night before she died. How about you?"

Debra Sue looked at me directly and smiled. "I have too. I've also thought about conversations that Elyse and I had for over more than a year ago. I think Elyse was preparing us for each other and setting us up long before that Sunday evening in the hospital."

My grin must have filled my face! "You too? Do you remember that double chocolate cake she baked for that last Valentine's Day? She inscribed it with, 'We Have Our Hearts.' Remember?"

Debra Sue nodded vigorously and returned my smile broadly. "Do I remember? Of course! Last year, Elyse told me that someday she expected me to get married, and that I could have her wedding dress if I wanted it."

"Elyse suggested that we wait six months, but I think we should wait longer than that. No one else knows about our final conversation with Elyse."

Debra Sue nodded. "I think you're probably right. What about waiting until after next Easter?"

I nodded as well. "That sounds excellent. It will give us plenty of time to strategize and plan for the next phase of our lives."

The restaurant closed while we were still talking, and when we realized that our waiter was waiting for us to leave, I left him a generous tip and blessed him before we left. Just before going out the door, I kissed Debra Sue for the first of what would be countless times."

The months flew by. For her birthday, I gave Debra Sue a jeweled cross that had been passed down through my family, which Elyse had never worn because she seldom wore jewelry. We kept our plans to ourselves through Christmas, and we kept our romance under wraps almost until Easter. I had two weeks of vacation time coming, so I called John and Nancy Wells in Oakland, California, where they lived with their pet cheetah. Two weeks later, I invited a friend from seminary, Dennis Riverton, to preach for me. Debra Sue's parents knew what was happening, and they were there, along with a few dozens of her friends who "happened" to be in town.

During the second worship service, when it came time for the sermon, Dennis and I went to the center of the chancel, and Debra followed three of her friends down the center aisle. She was wearing the most beautiful lace wedding dress I had ever seen. I recognized it because Elyse had worn it twenty-five years earlier.

The Kansas City gossip lines must have burned up during those two weeks we were in California for our honeymoon. John and Nancy Wells met us at the airport and gave us the keys to a small new motor home. They told us they would expect us to return the motor home after our honeymoon. Debra Sue didn't want to drive it, so she navigated while I drove.

After spending two nights at Lodgepole Campground in Sequoia National Park, we started up Interstate 5. Debra Sue did a lot of the talking as I drove. "Frank, we have not talked much about having kids. I told you I was on the pill when we got back from Elyse's funeral. Do you want to have a second family? You have three grown children who attended our wedding, with your youngest still going to Wichita State. Abby will graduate next June, won't she?"

I nodded. "Right. I know you love children, and so do I, so if you want for us to have our own, I'll enjoy having them if you will." I glanced to my right and winked at her. "Let's pray about it."

Debra Sue nodded, then she looked at her watch. "We had an early breakfast, are you getting hungry?"

"I could definitely eat. What's our GPS say?"

Debra Sue touched the screen. "East of here, there's a place called Bill's that has five stars and is reasonably priced. It's east only a few miles. Shall we head into the hills? You'll need to take this next exit. It's in a town called 'Towne.'"

"Really? ... Okay."

Marrying Debra Sue opened my eyes to many things I'd not seen before. That lunch decision led us to go into Yosemite Valley, where a cancellation enabled us to stay two nights. It seemed as if God blessed us and spoke to us there in new ways.

Then, we drove north past Sacramento to Redding, before turning west towards the coast. We saw the redwoods in both the national and state parks, and later we headed south into the wine country.

When we returned to Oakland, we spent one night with John and Nancy Wells. John had a proposal. He wanted to build a church on a fifteen-acre parcel he had purchased at the top of a hill and overlooking the bay. He wanted Debra Sue and I to build the church. We said we would pray about it, and we did that night.

When they took us to the airport the next morning, we said that we were happy in Kansas City, but promised them we would continue to think about building a church and to pray. I was 52, and Debra Sue was 26. The idea of building a church from scratch excited her. I thought maybe I was getting too old to start something like that.

Debra Sue and I had no idea what was waiting for us in Kansas City, but I had stopped crying over Elyse before I went to sleep.

12

We arrived home amid a storm of gossip.

2.

Gossip Is Evil

I screamed into my pillow. It shook with my anger. I knew that time would lessen the pain. I knew I had to forgive for the sake of my health, but future forgiveness could not lessen the present pain or anger. I will remember, but the pain will fade. I must bridle my tongue.

Debra Sue and I returned on a Wednesday so that we could catch up on our work before Sunday, and so we could put some of the jet-lag behind us. Harry Elliott, the chairman of our elders took me aside after the second service. "Pastor Frank, while you and Debra Sue were in California, the gossip mills have worked up to a fever pitch."

"Really! Do you think if I preached a sermon on gossip, that it would help? The wedding was not a total surprise, in that everyone could see our friendship blossoming into romance."

Harry offered me a wry smile. "A Biblical sermon on gossip certainly cannot hurt, but the whispers are mostly based upon lies, and some of the stories attributed to the two of you sound pretty nasty."

I nodded solemnly. "Do you want to move the Elders meeting up a week to this Tuesday night?"

Harry shook his head. "I think it would be better if we wait and see how the congregation responds to your next sermon."

Again, I nodded. "Okay."

Going back for many years in Kansas City, the usual routine was to eat dinner out on Sundays after church. Though Elyse was no longer with us, we still didn't want to work on preparation or cleanup. We just wanted to relax and eat slowly after working all morning. That Sunday we went to Q39, one of our favorite restaurants. I got the smoked and char-grilled half chicken, and Debra Sue ordered the Angus Beef Brisket.

After we had put our soups and salads where they belonged, our main courses came. I spoke quietly. "I talked to Harry, the chairman of the Elders, after church. The gossip mills have been churning furiously over us."

"I know. Lettie, your secretary, told me. I trust her completely, as you do. She filled me in."

"I've agreed to preach a sermon on gossip next Sunday."

She chewed some brisket and swallowed. "I'm not surprised you want to meet this head on. You shun passivity."

I think I tried to smile. "I'm not known as being shy when facing tough issues."

She looked directly at me, with a twinkle in her eyes. "You're not going to burn down the church with hellfire and brimstone, are you?"

My grunted response was almost a chuckle. "I suppose not, but there's plenty of Biblical material to work with. Do you feel like spending some time with me on our knees, discussing this thoroughly with Jesus?"

She swallowed some sweet tea. "Probably more than once."

Despite the gossip, we weren't worried about what might be ahead. We lingered over our dinner almost two hours, talking about anything that came to mind.

That evening, there were no emails for either of us, but the social media were active. The usual number of trolls were there, but per usual, we ignored them. We watched a couple of old videos of The Red Skelton Show, so we had some good laughs before retiring for the night.

My Monday morning office routine after a time of prayer was to come up with a sermon title for the following Sunday as soon as possible. At the latest, I would announce it at our Tuesday morning staff meeting. Our business manager took care of the church's administrivia. Regarding gossip, I did not want a clever or flippant title. I chose, "A Whisperer's Heart."

I quickly decided not to use the ninth commandment.

"You shall not give false testimony against your neighbor.
[Exodus 20:16 (NIV)]

I also decided not to use the Apostle Paul's proscription in his letter to Rome.

> *They have become filled with every kind of wickedness, evil, greed and depravity. They are full of envy, murder, strife, deceit and malice. They are gossips, slanderers, God-haters, insolent, arrogant and boastful; they invent ways of doing evil; they disobey their parents; they have no understanding, no fidelity, no love, no mercy.*
>
> [Romans 1:29-31 (NIV)]

This seemed to be much too harsh of a selection for the message that I wanted to deliver.

Early on Tuesday morning, shortly after 7:00 AM, I went into our sanctuary to pray. For nearly a half hour I sat there silently, hoping that God would reveal something to me. I gradually began to be aware of the Lord's presence and power. The words *Proverbs* and *Matthew* began to nudge the back of my mind. I pondered those two words – those two books – for about an hour. I took out my cell phone and opened up the Hebrew text of the Book of Mishlei (Proverbs). In chapter 26 I found the appropriate passage. I smiled and nodded, remembering the English New International Version.

> *Without wood, a fire goes out; without a gossip, a quarrel dies down. As charcoal to embers and as wood to fire, so is a quarrelsome person for kindling strife. The words of a gossip are like choice morsels; they go down to the inmost parts.*
>
> [Proverbs 26:20 (NIV 2011)

I began to relax, and I remembered how Jesus spoke about accountability for what we say. In the Greek text in a Bible application on my cell, I found what I was looking for in Matthew's Gospel. Translating it in my mind, I then looked for a published translation in English that I liked.

> *A good man brings good things out of the good stored up in him, and an evil man brings evil things out of the evil stored up in him. But I tell you that everyone will have to give account on the day of judgment for every empty word they have spoken. For by your words you will be acquitted, and by your words you will be condemned."*
>
> [Matthew 12:35-37 (NIV)]

16

It was nearly 10:00 AM when I finished praying and left the sanctuary. I went to my office via its private door, and I turned on the lights. I heard a knock on my main door. "Come in!"

My secretary came in. Lettie was my secretary since my first days at the church. Debra Sue loved her as much as Elyse had. "Good morning, Pastor Frank." You've been praying more than usual this morning."

I nodded. "Yes, the Lord has been helping get started on next Sunday's sermon. It will be called, 'A Whisperer's Heart.' Be sure to get this onto our web page. Tell George the morning's theme will be centered on authentic love, and to pick music revolving around love and joy."

"Okay. You have had three calls. They're under your paperweight. Grace Schumer is in U.K. Hospital. She's had a stroke."

"Didn't she have a stroke a few years ago?"

Lettie nodded. "Yes, about fifteen years ago, I think."

"All right, I'll pay her a visit after lunch. Is anything else pressing?"

"Debra Sue told me about Grace being in the hospital. She said to tell you that she suggests that the two of you see Grace together after lunch."

"Okay, Lettie, is there anything else?"

She shook her head. "There are just those three calls."

I nodded, "Okay."

She left, closing the door.

* * *

I knew Grace a long time. The first time I visited with her in her home, I learned that she was a gossip, and she declared that her gossip was "harmless." Of course, in the Garden of Eden, the serpent convinced Eve that the forbidden fruit was harmless, but it was still forbidden. It's easy for the Father of Lies to convince a gossip that their gossip is harmless.

Grace had found that being in "the loop" can be seductive and stepping out of it is a difficult call because gossip is an all-too-common currency of human connection. She simply could not believe that her gossip was keeping her in spiritual bondage to the Father of Lies.

As Debra Sue and I drove towards the hospital we talked about her. "You know, of course, that Grace is one of our worst gossips."

"Definitely!" She was emphatic. "When she's at our church women's luncheons, it is almost impossible to get her to stop gossiping."

"At Pepperdine, I heard several stories of how churches had been destroyed by well-intentioned gossips. Many pastors have burned out trying to cope with it. I'm thinking maybe we can take the risk of confronting it head-on with Grace."

Debra Sue nodded. "I'm thinking the same thing. She often tries to get me to share gossip with her, so I could lead off and tell her about Elyse's preparing us for each other."

"Good idea. You lead, off, and I'll butt in periodically."

It was shortly after 2:00 when Debra Sue and I arrived at the University of Kansas Hospital. When we got to Grace's room, she was sitting up in bed and watching a video. When she saw us at the door, she muted the sound. "Hi! I was hoping I'd see at least one of you today."

"Hello, Grace, how are you doing?"

She nodded. "So far, so good."

Debra Sue took over. "It's good you have a positive attitude, Grace."

The woman looked at her. "When did the two of you get back from your honeymoon?"

Debra Sue smiled. "We got back on Wednesday. As much as I could picture Elyse enjoying California with us, we had to get back to work."

"So, you thought about Elyse while you two were on your honeymoon?"

We both nodded, as Debra Sue continued. "Of course. "Elyse was preparing us for each other and setting us up long before she died."

Grace's eyes got big. "Really! How?"

"Last year, Elyse told me that someday she expected me to get married, and that I could have her wedding dress if I wanted it."

"I didn't know that!"

I nodded. "On Valentine's day of last year, Elyse baked a double chocolate cake inscribed it with, 'We Have Our Hearts.' We'll never forget that!"

Again, Grace's eyes got big. "That sounds like Elyse."

Again, I nodded. "We've never told anyone about our last conversation with Elyse. I guess it won't hurt to tell you about it. What do you think, my love?"

She gave me a wink that Grace could not see. "Sure! We were both shocked by what she proposed, so maybe Grace would be shocked as well!"

"Tell me!" Her eyes lit up.

Debra started slowly. "After the three of us worshiped, that Sunday evening, Elyse was upbeat, although her voice was quite weak. She said, 'I'm going to be going home soon.' I smiled. I asked what the doctor had said, but that wasn't what she meant, and she shook her head. She said she was not talking about Kansas City home, but rather that she was talking about her home in heaven."

Grace's mouth dropped open slightly. "That woman was always very intuitive, and she seemed centered on God somehow."

I nodded. "I had seen it coming for more than a week, and I asked her if maybe she could spring back again, but she was adamant. Her exact words were, 'No, Frank. I know I won't. That's why I wanted the two people I love the most here to worship with me this evening.' At that moment, I felt that the conversation might be our last, and it was."

Debra Sue nodded. "I knew it too. I began to cry. I told her I was not ready for her to go. I remember her response. It was, 'I know, love, but you know as well as I do that all that God does, God does well. It's time. You love my Frank, don't you?' Momentarily I was floored!"

Grace nodded solemnly. "I would be too!"

"I told Elyse that yes, except for Jesus, that Frank was the best friend I've ever had. Grace, if you're thinking 'friends with benefits,' you're wrong." Debra Sue was emphatic.

I nodded. "She then asked if I love Debra Sue, and I told her that she was like a precious daughter to me. After all, our children have seen her that way, and a few times they've even referred to her as 'sis.'"

Debra Sue grinned. "They have, and I've loved it! It was then that Elyse dropped her bomb on us."

Grace raised her brows, wide-eyed. "A bomb?"

Debra Sue nodded. "Her exact words were, 'When I return to heaven, I don't want either of you to be alone, and I think you will need each other when I'm gone.' We were both totally dumbfounded."

I nodded. "I tried to say something, but Elyse shushed me. She said that after she was buried, she expected us to wait for six months or so, and then we were to get married."

Again, Grace's mouth hung open. "You're kidding!"

Debra Sue grinned. "I told her she couldn't possibly mean it. She said she was serious, and then she talked about John Wells, and how he wanted to build a church in Oakland, and that we should go to San Francisco for our honeymoon."

I nodded. "Elyse told me that if Debra Sue wouldn't marry me, that I should take care of her, and made me promise to do so. Actually, on our honeymoon we hardly saw San Francisco at all." I paused. "Grace, there have been a couple of times when I've tried to get you to repent of your gossip, haven't I?"

Grace nodded. "You have, but I think my gossip is harmless, and I don't think the Lord minds."

"In the Garden of Eden, when the Devil told Eve that the forbidden fruit was harmless, was the fruit still forbidden?" Grace was silent. I took an envelope out of my pocket. "I've printed out the scriptures I'm preaching on this Sunday for you. All I ask is that you pray about them between now and Sunday morning." I handed her the envelope."

"Okay."

"Before we leave, let's pray together." I took Grace's good hand, and Debra Sue put her hand on top. "Heavenly Father, we lift Grace up to you. We know that only your Son Jesus saves, and he saves when we repent. Please help Grace be healed, not merely of her stroke, but help her to be healed spiritually as well. We ask in the precious name of Jesus. Amen."

We said our good-byes. In the elevator, Debra Sue spoke quietly. "Well, do you think we said too much?"

I kissed her on the cheek. "Time will tell. If all of this back-fires on us, there's always Oakland."

She nodded. "There's always Oakland, and this is only Tuesday."

Wednesday morning, my secretary, Lettie, greeted me in the reception area when I got to the office. "Good morning, Pastor Frank." She was pouring a cup of coffee for herself in one corner.

Our routine continued as usual. "Good morning, Lettie, did you sleep well?"

She turned and smiled, taking a sip from a steaming mug. "About as usual, I guess. Have you been on the Internet and checked the social media this morning?"

I shook my head. "Since Sunday, I've only barely kept up with email. Why, what's going on?"

"I don't know if I should be laughing or crying, but someone tweeted a question, asking if a Kansas City church should keep their pastor after he flies to California with his wife and Christian Education director and has three-way sex in San Francisco."

My eyes almost burst out of their sockets. "You've got to be kidding!"

Lettie nodded. "It's been re-tweeted thousands of times, and the trolls are having a field day. Several people pointed out that his wife was in a coffin, and that he and others were there a year ago to have a private burial service at a family cemetery plot. There have even been a few attempts to discuss necrophilia."

I shook my head. "Dear Lord in Heaven!"

The phone rang. "I'll get it." Lettie returned to her desk, and I went to my desk and sat down. I was stunned and stared out my window for several minutes.

"Pastor Frank, that call was from U.K. Hospital. Grace had a massive stroke a little while ago. She's gone. Her oldest daughter was there when she died, and she's the one who just called. She asked if she could see you this evening, and I told her your calendar was clear. She'll call back in a while to set up a time."

"Wow!" I picked up my phone's handset and punched buttons. "Hey, it's me."

My bride's voice was serious. "I'm not surprised. Did Lettie tell you about the Internet buzz?"

"Yes, and Grace has just died."

They were both silent for a moment. Debra Sue's voice was quieter. "Wow. I mean, well, I guess that's all I can think of to say."

"Right. Grace's daughter, Prudy Schumer-Bradley, will call later to make an appointment to see me, probably this evening."

"All of her family lives in this area. I wonder if there'll be a funeral this week, or whether they will postpone it until next week."

I had a feeling of resignation. "We'll know soon enough. We'll talk later. I love you."

"I love you too."

The meeting took place the next morning. Wyandotte-Holton Funeral Home is next to the lake. I met with five members of the family there, along with the home's director, Chip Holton. Chip was an old friend, and he remained silent unless family members addressed him specifically.

Grace's daughter, Prudy, seemed anxious to do all the talking. "Pastor Frank, I know that you and Debra Sue visited my Mom yesterday afternoon. When Mom started telling me about your visit yesterday evening, I stopped her twice to make sure that she wasn't just gossiping. I'm not a gossip, and Mom and I had a pact where we always told each other the absolute truth. It dates back to my teen years. Anyway, did Lady Elyse really set you and Debra Sue up to be married before she died?"

There was hushed silence as I nodded. "Yes, your Mom asked us about our honeymoon, and she was interested in how our romance developed. We told her the truth. I understand she had a stroke yesterday morning."

Prudy nodded. "I had helped her eat some breakfast while we were watching local news on streaming video. I sat down beside her, and when that absurd viral Internet story was being reported, I glanced at Mom. Her eyes were wide, but she wasn't moving. I became alarmed and called for the nurse. She never spoke again. I'll never know for sure, but I think that when she saw that horrible twisted and evil version of your story being reported, that triggered the end for her."

I nodded. "I doubt that you want to discuss my story right now. I already planned to preach on gossip this Sunday. What are you planning for her memorial or funeral?"

Prudy shook her head. "There won't be a funeral or a casket. Mom is being cremated." She looked around the room. "None of us except Bill have to work this weekend, and he can probably get the day off. I think we'd like to do a memorial service for Mom at the church on Saturday morning. Will that be okay?"

I nodded. "How about 10:00 AM? Will that be acceptable for you?"

Prudy looked around at the others, and they all nodded. She turned to me. "A mid-morning service was pretty much we talked about." She looked up at Chip. "Mr. Holton, may we have the urn of ashes and the flowers arranged by then? My oldest brother is putting together a video for the church's projection screens."

Chip nodded. "We'll help you will all of that. 10:00 AM will be fine.

Prudy looked at me again. "Pastor Frank, there's one more thing I need to say on behalf of all of us." Her eyes scanned the family, and they were all nodding. "We all loved my mother dearly. Several of us tried to get her to understand that gossip is evil, but she would not listen. Until the end, she believed that because she labeled her gossip as harmless that it was not evil. I have no doubt that when my mother saw on video what the Internet trolls were saying about you and Debra Sue, that her blood pressure went up sky high, and that caused her fatal stroke."

Tears were running down her cheeks as she paused. "Pastor Frank, we're all in agreement on this. When discussing gossip, we don't want you to pull any punches regarding my mother's gossip and gossip's evil nature. We all love you, and we trust your judgment. Mom is in God's hands."

Prudy glanced around at her family. "Does anybody want to add to that or to disagree?" They all shook their heads. "Okay, Pastor Frank. We'll see you Saturday morning." She stood up, and so did the rest of the family.

3.

Tears and Farewells

So often we knelt on our bed together to pray. This time our pillows were wet, but our eyes were finally dry. Our first few months of marriage had brought many painful episodes of rumors and gossip, and it was hard to leave Kansas City, but we were looking forward to life in California.

It was a habit for me to get to the church an hour or two before I had to be in the office. I treasured that silent time with God. Sometimes I prayed in the sanctuary, but when the weather was too cold, and it was too chilly there, I prayed in my office.

More than a year earlier, Lettie told me that she had kept a deceased cousin's accounts on the social media open, so she could "lurk" without others knowing she was there. She routinely scanned the pages of the more active members of the church.

Her deceased cousin's name was Tom Johnson, a very common name, and Lettie had changed his last address to Nome, Alaska, where he had never lived. Lettie had given me his username and password, so we could both "lurk" using the account. All we had to do was ignore friend requests, along with any messages. There were seldom any messages. Lettie and I agreed never to post anything to the account. We also agreed not to tell anyone else about our secret. Tom Johnson was a useful alias at times. Tom was also a convenient anonymous source of information.

The morning after my meeting with Grace's family, "Tom" logged in on each of his accounts to read the latest gossip. Some of it made me cringe. Some of it could not be shared with Debra Sue because I did not want her to be hurt. What I learned through Tom gave me even more to pray about.

The Saturday morning memorial service was not well attended. Grace made quite a few enemies during her lifetime. One woman quietly told me that she came just to be sure that Grace was dead. I shook my head. "For your own sake, you have to forgive her." She scowled.

Sunday morning came quickly enough. I preached as though I had the Bible open in one window of my computer, and the social media in another. I explained the inner psychology of gossips or "whisperers." I demonstrated how Jesus may well have been history's first and best psychoanalyst. I talked about how gossips deceive themselves, and towards the end, I talked about what the Bible says about people who intentionally do evil, as well as our need to forgive.

I emphasized how, even though we're told that telling lies about our neighbors is wrong, gossips continue to believe that their fabrications are *harmless*. Near the beginning of the Bible, we're told how the serpent convinced Eve that the forbidden fruit was *harmless*. The fruit was still forbidden, of course. I closed with a prayer on behalf of gossips, along with a prayer for their victims.

Debra Sue and I went to The Tropical Chicken for lunch. We love having their air-fried plantain strips instead of French fries. My beautiful bride was upbeat. "If I were a betting woman. I'd bet you're glad that sermon is behind you!" She winked.

I nodded. "I suppose so, although after doing Grace's memorial service yesterday, my sermon this morning flowed more easily than I expected. I'm not exactly looking forward to the monthly meeting of the Elders tomorrow."

She chewed some chicken strips and washed them down with Dr. Pepper. "Most of it will probably be about the gossip, I would imagine."

Between plantain strips, I nodded again. "It may well turn out that way, although Harry Elliott, our Elders chairman, says there's a second thorny issue that has to be discussed. He hasn't told me what it is."

She smiled. "I guess this will be one of those times when I want to hear about what is said, and you won't be able to share with me."

"That's true, but I don't tell them about all of our conversations either. I winked back at her."

Both of us took that Monday off. After dropping me off at Powell Gardens, she went to the K.C. Medical Center to get her annual physical. I spent most of the morning indulging my photography hobby. After seeing her doctor, Debra Sue did some shopping. As planned, she picked me up at the Gardens entrance at noon, and we headed for 'A Little Barbeque Joint' – where we'd had our first kiss about a year earlier.

With possible tornadoes in the forecast, after our noon dinner, we headed home. Behind our garage, Elyse and I had built a combination storm shelter and safe room that was rated to withstand an F5 storm. We kept our most valuable things there, but that day we didn't have to enter it. The warning siren never went off. Debra Sue and I watched a couple of movies and relaxed.

As usual, Harry started the Elders meeting on time with a prayer. After Alex Tillerson, the oldest man, read the minutes from the previous month's meeting, Harry led things off. "We have two things on the agenda this evening. We could spend all night talking about gossip, yesterday's sermon, and what lies ahead, but I'm going to save that for last." He paused and looked at Gary Goodyear, the youngest elder, who was in his early thirties.

"Gary, I have to ask you a question. I don't like asking, but I have to ask. While Pastor Frank and Debra Sue were on their honeymoon in California, I attended a seminar at the Hyatt Regency. I saw something that made me look twice, to make sure I wasn't mistaken. Two months ago, my wife and I saw you in the distance at the Country Club Plaza while we were shopping, and we were puzzled. Then, at the Hyatt Regency, I saw you kissing Alicia Corning after having seen you holding hands with her previously at the mall." Gary's eyes got big. "What's going on, Gary?"

All the color drained from the young man's face, and he looked down. He spoke very quietly. "Since I cannot avoid answering your question, all of you might as well hear the whole story." He paused and swallowed. "Alicia and I grew up together. We never dated. We were simply good friends. When I married Tonia, I was head over heels in love with her, and I still am. Alicia was one of the bridesmaids, and we had nothing but friendship."

Gary swallowed hard, struggling to express himself. "Shortly after Tonia and I celebrated our first anniversary, Tonia had a one-night stand with a former boyfriend from high school. I went crazy. We separated for over a month, and Alicia began listening to my troubles. As you know, Alicia's husband, Bart, is a long-haul trucker, and he's gone for two weeks or more at a time. You don't need to hear the details as to how it happened, but she and I began an affair. I guess it was because we were both lonely." He coughed, and then he sighed.

I got a bottle of water out of my office fridge and gave it to Gary, and he continued. "Meanwhile, Tonia and I missed each other terribly, and over a period of several months, we worked things out and got back together. Soon after that, Tonia got pregnant the first time. Alicia was still our friend, and Tonia had no clue as to what had started with Alicia while Tonia and I were separated."

Harry asked quietly, "So, you and Alicia have continued to see each other?"

Gary nodded, sheepishly. "Usually, we don't get together more than once or twice a month, but during both of Tonia's pregnancies, we saw each other two or three times a week."

I was shocked. "Did you say, 'Two or three times *a week?*'"

"Yes. I guess I should resign from being an elder."

Harry nodded. "And you should do more. You know that the affair must end, and you know that you need to tell Tonia."

Gary stood up. "I'll put my resignation in writing, and I'll leave now."

I stood up and stopped him. "I understand why you want to leave now, and we have no right to hold you back, but please let us pray for you first."

"Okay." Ten men put our hands upon Gary's shoulders, and we prayed for him several minutes.

"Gary," I told him, "I expect to see you Sunday. How you handle this is in your hands. What has been said here is between us." He didn't say another word. After Gary left, we took a break before continuing.

Harry later continued to speak quietly. "We've been here only a short time, and already I'm exhausted! Does anyone want to speak specifically about either the gossip of the last several weeks or Pastor Frank's sermon yesterday?" He looked around the room.

At first, the other eight men were silent. Alex Tillerson looked up from his notes as recording secretary. "Yesterday, Pastor Frank, I was once again glad that you're our pastor." As I closed my eyes and nodded he continued before I could respond. "You handled the subject of gossip Biblically, and you did so with far more dignity and grace than I could ever muster within myself."

Several of the men nodded, saying, "Amen."

Alex started to write down what he had said, and then he put his pen down. "I've got to say one more thing. I've known John and Nancy Wells since they were in high school in this church, and I was one of their sponsors. I know about their request to have you and Debra Sue start a church for them in Oakland." He paused and looked straight at me. "Frank, if you and Debra Sue go to Oakland, don't do it because of this consarned gossip. If you and Debra Sue leave, do it only if both of you are convinced that God is calling you two out there. Tell her I said so." He looked around the room.

Harry nodded. "This part of our meeting can and should be shared with her, does everyone agree?" They all nodded. For over an hour, we discussed what may lie ahead for the church.

When I got home, I told Debra Sue everything that had been said during the second half of the meeting.

* * *

Late Saturday morning, we were watching a news summary when a bell appeared in the lower-left corner of our giant-screen display. Debra Sue touched the remote, and the news summary was replaced by John and Nancy Wells in their living room filling the screen. We both smiled. "Well! Good morning!"

John looked at his watch. "I imagine you two will be having lunch soon, but we slept in and have only just finished breakfast. Is this a good time for you to talk?"

Debra Sue grinned. "Sure! We like to take Saturdays off, like a traditional Sabbath, so we've not scheduled anything today. What's up?"

Nancy smiled. "A lot of people have been praying about having a church up on the hill that John and I bought. We have some further details to give you, with the hope that we can encourage you to say yes."

John held up a large mailing tube. "Inside this is a master plan for the fifteen acres of property we've acquired, along with city-approved blueprints for three buildings. The best church architect in the country, Leroy Wright, has laid this all out."

Nancy nodded. "We talked to the management of two hotels about using a large room on Sunday mornings, but the best facilities are too far away from the Oakland hills. Then we found a funeral home that has a large chapel. They are willing to let us use it every Sunday morning as a tax right-off for them. We've started advertising a new-church start but have not committed to a temporary location yet. Please pray about this more! We're ready to get started!"

As I look back at that moment, there were hundreds of thoughts going through my mind. Deep down, though, I almost concluded right then that Debra Sue and I were probably headed there. I didn't let on. "We'll pray about it, of course. I – we – understand that you've been talking to our oldest Elder, Alex Tillerson."

John and Nancy looked at each other. John nodded. "We agree with Alex on that. If you don't have a sense of call here from the Lord, then we can't push you. It has to be the Lord's call. As far as finances are concerned, the land for the new church is free and clear, and there are already invested donations to cover your salaries, benefits, and expenses for at least the first year."

"Wow! Thank you both!" Debra Sue looked at me. "Frank and I are going to have to discuss this more as well as pray about it. We've made you wait, and that's not fair to you."

John shook his head. "Don't worry about that. If all of this is according to God's will, it will happen. Let's talk again next weekend, shall we?"

I nodded. "Okay, and meanwhile we'll be praying even more about it. Bye."

Debra Sue smiled. "Bye."

They said good-bye and ended the call. The video screen returned to the news summary we had been watching. Debra Sue muted the sound.

I looked at my bride. "They are making it seem easier to leave, but I'm still not sure it is what God wants us to do. You've been here a relatively short time, but I've been here more than a quarter of a century – most of my adult life. What do you think?"

She leaned over and kissed my cheek. "I love you, Frank, and I know this greater Kansas City area is part of who you are because you've lived here twenty-five years longer than I have. I understand why this must be so difficult for you. You're right, I don't think leaving here will be difficult for me. The idea of you and I making a fresh start is very appealing."

I nodded. "Making a fresh start is appealing to me, but our making a big move can be really exhausting. Let's look at the pros and cons."

"Okay. The idea of my being closer to friends and family is appealing to me, but I wouldn't be moving for them. Your children and the rest of your family are scattered all over. That's not an issue."

I nodded. "I agree. We'll be growing a new church, and we will be growing our own new relationships, and the resulting growing pains can be challenging, but I'm not really concerned, are you?"

Debra Sue shook her head. "No. Oakland has a more cosmopolitan and progressive culture, and for me that is both exciting and a little scary. If God is calling us there, we'll be leaning on the Lord constantly."

I smiled. "I trust the Lord totally, and I think you do too. If the Lord is calling us to Oakland, we'll be leaving behind the Kansas City gossips, but we will gain the Oakland gossips. We'll be leaving behind some precious friends, but we will be making new friends. That issue is a wash, don't you think?"

She nodded. "Definitely. The crime rate is definitely higher in California, but you and Elyse taught me to surrender such concerns to the Lord. Can we put this on the back burner until tomorrow evening? I'll be helping with the breakfast for the children tomorrow morning, and you have a full day."

I nodded. "I agree, let's let go of this until after tomorrows routines. When John told us that the finances for the first year are already set up, that gave me an idea for an extra illustration for tomorrow's sermon on stewardship."

We stood up and began preparations for our nightly chores and routines.

Every morning, our bedroom's streaming video monitor comes on at 5:00 AM with a newscast. Usually, we watch for 10-15 minutes, until we're wide awake, and then we turn it off to worship. That Sunday morning, my cell phone rang before the television came on. It was Gary Goodyear. "Hey, Gary, you and Tonia aren't usually awake at this time. What's up?"

"Tonia's here in the Emergency Room at the K.C. Clinic."

"Really! What happened?"

"She got up to go to the bathroom a little over an hour ago, and she began breathing very rapidly, and she told me she felt horrible and couldn't breathe."

"Okay Gary," I said, "I'll get dressed and be there as soon as I can."

"Thanks, Pastor Frank." He hung up.

I looked over at Debra Sue, who was awake. "That was Gary Goodyear. He's at the K.C. Clinic, and from what he told me, it sounded like Tonia was having a panic attack. I'll dress and go over there, and then, depending upon how long I'm with them, I'll possibly eat breakfast in the clinic's cafeteria and go on to the church." I leaned over, kissed Debra Sue, and started getting out of bed.

"Okay, I'll worship and pray, and then I'll be okay here with doing my usual stuff and head for the church. I'll see you there." The television came on. She reached for the remote and muted it. "Tell them I'm praying for them."

I've had many emergency calls like that over the years, so it did not take me long to shave, shower, dress, and head out the door. Less than twenty minutes after Gary's call, I was approaching him in the waiting room outside of the Emergency Ward. I shook his hand. "Good morning, Gary, what's the latest?"

"So far, they're still doing tests, but an electrocardiogram showed no heart problems. Thank God! All we can do is wait for the results of other tests, I guess."

We sat down. "How are you doing, Gary?"

"Okay, sort of." He paused. "After I left the Elders Meeting, I went home and told Tonia everything. She surprised me. She blames herself for my affair with Alicia. She says her affair with Ed Miller, her ex-boyfriend from high school, started all of this. I told her not to blame herself, and we've talked constantly since then, about things we've not discussed in a long time. I thought we were doing okay and getting through that crisis, and now this has happened."

I nodded. "Until we hear the results of her tests, we don't know, do we?"

Gary shook his head. "No. We told the ER doctor briefly about what has been going on, and he said that what she is experiencing might be a panic attack."

"What you described to me on the phone sounded like that."

Gary nodded. "Thanks for understanding, Pastor Frank, and for being here."

A door opened, and a nurse approached us. "Mr. Goodyear, you can come back and be with her again now." She led us through the door and down a corridor.

As we went behind a curtain, Tonia looked up from a gurney and tried to smile. "Hello, Pastor Frank, I'm glad you're here."

A woman in green scrubs and a white coat came in and greeted us. "Good morning." She looked at me. "Good morning, Pastor Frank, I'm on duty all day today, so I won't be in church this morning. Gary, Tonia's tests are all okay. I'm admitting her to a private room so that this afternoon, she will meet with Dr. Trina Battanski, our psychiatrist on call this weekend." She looked at Tonia. "Don't worry, I don't think this is anything truly serious, but I want Dr. Battanski to evaluate what has been going on in your life, okay?"

Tonia nodded. "I understand. In fact, I think it's a good idea."

I nodded. "I'm glad you're willing to talk it out with a professional. Debra Sue and I will be praying for you. Before I leave, I'll offer a prayer here." I looked at the doctor. "Sylvia, it's a blessing that you're the doctor on duty this morning, because you know everyone here. I also know Dr. Battanski. Two years ago, she and I led a workshop for pastors, updating their pastoral counseling skills."

"Will I be staying overnight?" Tonia's eyebrows were up.

The doctor shook her head. "I doubt it, Tonia, but that is up to Dr. Battanski. Just relax for now. An orderly will be coming to wheel you upstairs in a few minutes." She looked at Tonia's husband. "Gary, you could go up with her to the room, but I suggest that you go to church instead. Dr. Battanski will call you after she has seen Tonia, okay?"

He forced a smile. "Okay." He looked at me. "Will you pray with us first?"

I did so, and Gary kissed Tonia on the cheek before he left. I went into the cafeteria to eat breakfast.

4.

New Beginnings

The next five weeks pass with a roller coaster of emotions, challenges, and blessings. There would be thirty-nine days after Tonia's panic attack, before we would be standing in the living room of our new home in Oakland. Debra Sue and I would look around at our hastily-placed furniture, with boxes stacked high. Debra Sue would be grinning. Much would have to happen first.

Tonia went home that evening. She and Gary had an appointment for their first marriage counseling session with Dr. Battanski. They hoped they could make a fresh start.

The following Sunday, Sylvia greeted Debra Sue with a hug, and then she turned to me. "Your sermon this morning was just what I needed to hear. Jack and I," she looked at her husband, "agree that I've got to start keeping the Sabbath. From this day forwards, we're going to do our best to have either Sunday or Wednesday off together, so that we can rest, have some fun, and worship together. By the way, I'm sure you are as pleased as I am that things turned out so well since last Sunday morning." She smiled.

I nodded. "Yes! God is good, always. If you and Jack are interested in being more involved in our congregation's life, just let us know."

"We will!" They started moving towards the parking lot, but they were stopped by some friends.

Debra Sue and I glanced briefly after them, and then we re to greeting others leaving the sanctuary.

That evening, we were eating some peach cobbler à la mode when Debra Sue muted the television. "We've decided, haven't we? It's been pretty easy for me, but you're through struggling, aren't you?"

I smiled and kissed her. "Yes, my love, I no longer have any misgivings about moving to Oakland. If you want to have a pet cheetah like Sheila, I'm sure John and Nancy can get one for us."

She laughed. "O no! I love Sheila, and I love her purr – and I love cats, I really do!" She laughed again, "but I don't want a cat *that big!* After we get moved in, let's get a couple of cats that will be strictly indoor cats, and get at least two, maybe three, so they can keep each other company when we're not home."

By that time, I was laughing too. "What? No dogs?"

She cocked her head to the side. If we have a fenced back yard, maybe we can have a nice big dog who can play outside."

"Okay, maybe, but…." A chime sounded in the muted TV.

Debra Sue reached for the remote, and John and Nancy Wells were on the screen. "Good evening!" John and Nancy said it together.

Debra Sue smiled and nodded. "Good evening! Frank and I have just finished some peach cobbler à la mode, and we were talking about our decision to move to Oakland."

John smiled. "Great! So, you're accepting God's call to Oakland?"

I nodded and smiled as well. "Yes! We can announce our sense of call to Oakland next Sunday. I think we can probably be there before the end of August." I looked at beloved Debra Sue. "What do you think?"

She nodded. "If we can get there by the middle of August, we might be able to have our first worship service on the day before Labor Day."

Both John and Nancy nodded. John was excited. "Excellent! Nancy had a brainstorm last week that might appeal to you."

She shifted, sharing John's excitement. "We can worship in the funeral home chapel when the weather demands it, but so long as the weather is nice, the top of the hill has already been leveled, with plenty of room for parking. We could set up a circus-sized tent with a small stage for a praise team. We can also erect a storage building to store chairs, tables, and other necessities. What do you think?"

Debra Sue shared in their excitement. "We'll pray about it of course, but I think that would be a great way to start, don't you, Frank?"

Perhaps I was overly thoughtful when I nodded. "This sounds good, but as Debra Sue says, we'll pray about it. She and I will have a lot to deal with over the next few weeks as we move towards this calling."

Nancy nodded. "Our guest suite with kitchenette will be yours until you get into a house. Debra Sue, I got your letter, so I know what you'll be hoping for in a house. I'll get a realtor started on it tomorrow morning. We'll leave it to you to have a realtor there in Kansas to coordinate with ours, okay?"

"Okay. I'm going to leave it to Frank to get any of our church stuff packed up and moved, and I'll take care of things here at home, okay Frank?"

I smiled and nodded. "Right! I love having a youngster doing all the heavy lifting!" She leaned over and kissed me, as I continued. "Have the realtor on your end post emails to us that include pictures as well as all details of possible houses for us."

Debra Sue touched my hand. "John, when you showed us the property that you've secured for the church, you said something about having a parsonage on the same property. Was that just an off-hand comment?"

"No." He paused. "I realize that many pastors and their families don't like living on the church's property, and that's not what I meant." He paused, struggling for words. "If you recall, there are some large trees on the property and on the property surrounding it. When I first talked with our architect, Leroy Wright, he talked about building log post and beam homes in that area, to be in tune with the environment. He also said something about designing a unique church around that same idea. We dismissed that idea. There are several log post and beam homes being built within a half-mile of the church. If that appeals to you, I'll have the realtor include those among the possibilities."

With this information, Debra Sue was even more excited than before. "Yes! Yes! When Frank and I were on our honeymoon, we talked about – loving – the idea of living in a log home, but they don't fit into city-like environments. I hope the realtor can supply some virtual reality tours."

Nancy smiled. "I understand, but our church property is in a forested suburb environment. I'll share this idea with the realtor."

John looked at her and nodded. "Okay, we've got a lot to think about and pray about. Shall we talk again next Sunday, about the same time?"

I nodded, and we ended the call a few moments later.

+ + +

Even when I made it clear to the Kansas City congregation that Debra Sue and I felt God calling us to Oakland, there were many people who tried for a couple of weeks to convince us to stay. On the flip side of our decision, a very active member of the congregation, John Sinja, said his trucking company would provide a truck and workers, getting Debra Sue and me both loaded in Kansas and unloaded in Oakland. He wrote a letter to that effect, stating that he would take it off of his taxes as a charitable business expense. I publicly thanked him. (He would subsequently go on to tell me a year later that the publicity and increased business more than offset the cost of our move.)

Two weeks before we made our move, Debra Sue and I were taking a break to read the Sunday paper. Suddenly, she slammed the paper into her lap. "Wow! I thought our paper had pretty responsible reporters, but this is downright silly!"

I looked at her. "What's silly?"

The columnist, Malcolm Jeppley, says that you and I are being forced to move out of state because of Internet trolls and gossip!"

I goggled at her. "He's not a member of our church, but he's a regular member of Sam Bassett's church down the street. He should know better! Do you think I should call him?"

She shook her head. "I've a better idea. Isn't his wife's name Paula?"

"I think so, yes."

"I'll call her and invite her and her husband to join us for dessert this evening. I've got plenty of apricot cobbler."

I agreed. That evening, we were all sitting in our den, having cobbler, ice cream, or both. "Malcolm, the reason Debra Sue wanted to invite you and Paula over tonight, and I agreed, was because of your column in today's paper."

He nodded. "I thought that might be the case."

"Well Malcolm, I don't know what your sources are, and I don't care, but simply stated, you were wrong."

"How so?"

"When Elyse was still alive, John and Nancy Wells wrote to us from Oakland, telling us about their new home, about their purchasing land for a church in the Oakland Hills, and they invited Elyse and I to visit them in Oakland because they wanted us to help him start the new church on the property they had acquired."

"Really!" Paula was surprised.

"Yes, and in our last conversation with Elyse before she died, she told Debra Sue that after she was gone she wanted Debra Sue and I to get married and honeymoon in San Francisco."

Malcolm's mouth dropped open. "So, you're telling me that this is the reason why you're moving?"

I shook my head. "No, Malcolm. The whole idea was almost too incredible for us, but we agreed to pray about it. You're a Christ-centered man, so you know what the phrase 'praying it through' means."

"I've heard the expression, but I'm not sure how I would define it or describe it."

I nodded. "It means discussing it with God from all angles and perspectives, from both divine and human perspectives. It also means discussing with God all the pros and cons, including our own attitudes. Elyse wanted us to wait six months after she was in heaven before we got married, and we waited a year. We still were not convinced we should make the move. I confronted this community's gossip head on, both on Sundays and at other times, and I was praised for it. The Internet trolls thrive on getting attention, but I never addressed any of their garbage. I even told my congregation to ignore it. In short, Malcolm, you were totally wrong. God is calling us to Oakland to start a new church, and we're excited about going."

He nodded. "Okay. I'll eat humble pie in my next column. Do you want my retraction tomorrow, or shall I wait until next Sunday?"

I shook my head. "That's your business, whether you write a retraction or not or even when. I'll not ask you when I should preach what, and I won't tell you your business. We invited you and Paula over for dessert so that you can know the truth."

He grinned. "Thank you! You and Debra Sue are being very gracious."

Paula nodded. "Amen to that. Debra Sue, can we stay in touch?" My bride nodded. "I think that after your new church is built, that Malcolm and I could take a vacation out on the left coast, and we could see your church. Malcolm might want to write a follow-up column."

Her husband laughed. "I think this is the first time you've suggested something for me to write!"

She shook her head. "Not really, but it might turn out to be a good idea."

"True!" He smirked.

For the remainder of the evening, Malcolm and Paula wanted to hear more details about what was being planned for the Oakland hills.

I tossed and turned that night until I awakened enough to focus upon God's presence. As I was starting to breathe more deeply, the chorus of a Chris Tomlin song began to emerge in my mind.

> *My chains are gone*
> *I've been set free*
> *My God, my Savior has ransomed me*
> *And like a flood His mercy reigns*
> *Unending love, amazing grace*

I knew what I was going to preach about. I drifted back and forth from peaceful sleep to contented prayer.

Since I had prayed off and on through the night, after Debra Sue and I read scriptures the next morning, we prayed for one another. Then I was so energized, I almost skipped breakfast. The aromas of waffles and bacon talked me into eating.

I was working my computer's keyboard rapidly when Lettie unlocked her office and turned on the lights. She tapped on my door and walked in. "Good morning, Pastor Frank! You must not have prayed very long in the sanctuary before you started working. Did you know that Gary and Tonia are in there, praying now?"

I stopped and stared at Lettie. "I didn't go into the sanctuary this morning. Since Gary was an elder, he's got a key. I'm sure he'll turn it in when Harold asks him. It's good to know they're praying together." There was a soft knock on my outer office door. "Come in!"

It was Gary and Tonia, and I returned their greeting, "Good morning!" I turned to Lettie. "I'll give you my sermon title after I visit with Tonia and Gary." Lettie left and closed the door behind her. "Would you like to sit down?" They nodded and sat at my desk. "What can I do for you two this morning?"

Tonia spoke first. "Pastor Frank, we've decided that we have to forgive each other and ourselves, but we're not sure where to start."

"Yes! We love each other, but we also know we've painfully hurt each other. For Tonia, the pain is new, and for me, it is a lingering dull ache."

I said the first thing that came into my mind. "All that God does, God does well."

"What?" They said it almost together.

"Last night, I tossed and turned for a while, but as I usually do, once I was sufficiently awake, I began focusing upon God's presence. The old Chris Tomlin chorus began going through my mind, and I realized that the phrase *'my chains are gone, I've been set free,'* is going to be at the center of next Sunday's sermon on forgiveness. You two are definitely not the only ones who need to forgive and be forgiven."

Tonia cocked her head slightly. "So, you want us to listen to your sermon carefully this Sunday?"

I smiled. "I always want people to listen carefully to what God gives me to say, but you don't have to wait a week to have a bit of counsel. Speaking of which, how are things going with Dr. Battanski?"

They both nodded, and Gary took Tonia's hand. "She's great. She understands our pain, and she's been really helpful."

"Good. Whenever trust is violated, it is difficult and often painful to regain that trust. What's worse, when we don't forgive, our brain orders chemicals into our blood that, if they're not processed and eliminated, they are harmful to us physically. It's like taking poison and waiting for the other person to die. They're the same chemicals that empower us when we have to fight or run, so we have to either work hard physically, or change our attitude and let the remaining chemicals work their way out of our systems."

Gary nodded. "Wow! That makes sense! That's why, when Tonia cheated on me about a year after we got married, I felt like I was being eaten up inside."

Tonia vigorously nodded. "That's how I feel now."

"You two have been Christians for quite a while, so between now and next Sunday, your prayers can include talking to each other and God about Jesus and Judas." I had their attention. "Judas was part of Jesus' closest circle of friends. They were closer than brothers in most ways. We don't know why Judas did what he did. There have been countless attempts to speculate his reason or reasons. In the end, Judas violated Jesus' trust. Judas could not forgive himself, and that is where both of you must begin."

Tonia's mouth hung open slightly, and Gary said, "Say that again? You want us to begin, not with forgiving each other, but forgiving ourselves?"

I nodded. "Tonia, you have evidently never forgiven yourself for what you did long ago. Some might ask, how can you expect Gary to forgive you, if you cannot forgive yourself? Gary, you begin by forgiving yourself and repenting of what you did by having an affair so that Tonia can forgive you. Tonia, Gary's forgiveness of you for what you did so long ago was incomplete." I paused as we gazed at each other. "That's right. His forgiveness of you was incomplete because you had not forgiven yourself. Jesus came to Earth as an expression of God's desire to forgive and redeem."

I shifted and leaned forward at my desk. "While the nails were giving him agony, he said, *'Father, forgive them, because they don't know what they are doing.'* He forgave them anyway, even though it was not logical from a human point of view. The response of Jesus must be your response. Your goal is to forgive one another anyway, so that you can work towards trusting each other again. This is where you begin. Do you understand?"

They both nodded at me and at one another. Tonia spoke softly. "I think we understand."

"Good. It will not be easy. If you have the time, why don't the two of you go back into the sanctuary and talk for a while about Jesus and Judas? The Judas solution was the wrong one, but Jesus' forgiveness was the right one. When you're ready, try inviting Jesus into your conversation."

"Okay." Gary stood up, helping Tonia stand. "We'll see you Sunday." Tonia's eyes were moist as she nodded. As they left quietly, I realized that I had a lot of work to do on my sermon. Talking with them was a trial run of sorts.

I got up and went to my other door, into the church office. Lettie looked up as I walked in. I nodded my head towards the other door. "They'll be in the sanctuary a bit longer I think. As I was going to tell you before they came in, my sermon title will be 'My Chains Are Gone.' It will be about repentance, grace, and forgiveness. It might turn into two-part – or even a three-part – series. I'll know by Wednesday or Thursday."

"Okay. Are you going to do a column for the online newsletter this week?"

I nodded. "I'll probably give it to you tomorrow morning. Right now, I'm going to work a bit more on my outline for Sunday's sermon. Take messages from callers except for emergencies."

"Right." I turned, went back into my office, and closed the door.

I worked the rest of the morning on my sermon. A few minutes after noon, Debra Sue came by, and we went to lunch. As I recall, we decided on burgers and chocolate shakes. That's not important, though. We headed toward our house.

Pulling into our driveway, we were no longer as tired and hungry. As we came in the front door, we were greeted by a strange odor. Debra Sue reacted. "What in the world is that smell?!"

What happened next happened fast. Someone wearing a hood over their head came in from the dining room with a gun pointed at us. Before either of us could react, the gun was fired.

Beside me, Debra Sue started to crumple, and I saw blood in the middle of her chest. I screamed. "No!" and started to follow her down. As I looked at the shooter, the gun was being pointed at me. With no thought, I heard myself say, "In the name of Jesus, may the Earth swallow you and leave no trace."

The shooter began to drop through the floor, and a man's voice screamed. His arms went into the air, and he disappeared with his gun. I looked at Debra Sue, and her eyes were closed. I put my hands between her breasts over the bullet hole and the blood coming out. "Jesus! In your name, please deliver us from this evil." I closed my eyes, and time seemed to freeze.

Whether seconds or minutes passed, I don't know, but Debra Sue stirred beneath my hands. I opened my eyes, and her eyes were fixed on me. "Praise Jesus! I'm alive!" She sat up. "I'm alive! I was above you, watching that man drop through the floor into the Earth. Now, we're looking at each other. Blessed be Jesus' name and its power and authority!"

"Amen!" was all I could think of to say.

She began to unbutton her blood-soaked blouse, but there was no visible wound. "I'm healed! I'm healed, Frank! Praise God again! And again!" We stood and embraced. We held each other for a long time.

"Amen again!" She looked across the room and pointed. "That's where he shot me, and he's gone. Wow! I'm going to go get another blouse and put this one in the wash." She kissed me on the cheek and headed for the laundry room.

I went back out on the porch and looked around. There was no traffic, and none of our neighbors were outside where they could be seen. There was a car parked under the tree in front of our neighbors to the south, but no one could be seen.

I took out my phone and dialed 9-1-1. "Hello? This is Pastor Frank Frazee. I'm at 1741 Linden Avenue. My wife and I heard a loud noise, like a shot being fired, when we got home a few minutes ago, but now out here in front of my house, I don't see anything unusual. It seemed pretty loud when we were in our living room. Has anyone else reported hearing a shot fired in my neighborhood? There's a car parked in front of my neighbor's house that I don't recognize, but I don't see anyone."

I heard the screen door open behind me, and Debra Sue was there. She simply got closer and put an arm around me.

The 9-1-1 operator was calm and concise. "No other calls have come in, sir, but I'm dispatching a car to your neighborhood to check things out. Please stay on the line until the patrol car gets there. It should not be more than two or three minutes."

A police car arrived in less than five minutes. I repeated our story to them. They checked with our neighbors, both next to us and across the street. No one else heard the shot. The car was towed away. Five and a half weeks later, we were in Oakland after 1800 miles of westward driving, standing in our new living room, looking ahead to unpacking dozens of boxes. As we began to move in, Debra Sue and I seemed to always be smiling.

5.

Settling and Building

Moving into a new home is one thing. Building a new church from scratch is another. Whenever there's a divine plan, God must be trusted with the whole process.

Although we actually started driving west on Interstate 80 on a Monday morning, there was a last-minute decision made the previous Friday evening, when we were having our weekly conversation with John and Nancy. The moving van had left in the early afternoon on Friday, and we were relaxing in a motel just west of the city on Friday evening, where we would stay through the weekend.

Debra Sue was excited. "The van left the old house at about 2:30 this afternoon. We should be in Oakland by Thursday."

Nancy smiled. "Don't be in a hurry, you two, we'll be here whenever you arrive. There's been a development, though. John?" She looked at her husband.

"That's right. The house you've bought had its final inspection today, so you can move in as soon as you get here. The motorhome you drove on your honeymoon is parked in the driveway, so you have a place to stay while you get moved in."

I was surprised and glad. "That's fantastic! We've made great memories in that motorhome, and we can truly relax in it. Is it hooked up?"

Nancy nodded. "We've connected it to water, electricity, and the Internet, and if you're in it more than a few days, there's a dumping station less than two miles away."

Debra Sue was smiling. "We can easily handle that!"

John nodded. "The same movers who did an excellent job of moving Nancy and I in a few years ago are now contracted to move you into your new home. Your friend in Kansas City has arranged all of that. On the other front, everything is falling into place for the first Sunday in September."

I think I smiled at that. "I hope that Debra Sue and I are as ready for all of this as you and Nancy are!"

"No worries! Nancy and I will see you when you get here!" The call ended.

I looked at Debra Sue. "We don't need to tell John and Nancy about our home invasion, do we?"

She shook her head. "No. I agree. We don't need to tell them. There's a police report, but it only tells of talking to our neighbors. I'm completely healed, and a criminal has disappeared. The only two people in the world that know about our home invasion are looking at each other." She smiled. "We must have arrived just after he did. My jewelry box was on the bed and open, but nothing was missing. The erstwhile thief did not damage anything except a lock and a blouse, and we lost nothing. The thief's family, if he had one, lost him, but all of that is in God's hands."

I nodded. "I think we should seal that blouse in a plastic bag with the air sucked out, and then put it somewhere safe. We maybe will never look at it again, but also maybe someday it could be useful." I looked at her quizzically. "What do you think?"

"I washed it, but the blood stains are still on it. I left the hole alone. One of those gallon-sized vacuum-seal food storage bags ought to be big enough. When we move in, I will put it at the bottom of a drawer or behind something on a seldom-used shelf."

I nodded. "I'm looking forward to seeing our house in person. The 3-D images and virtual reality videos helped, but being there will be much better. I don't really like virtual reality software."

She grinned. "That's your age and your generation talking! I grew up with it, so I have no problem with it!"

On Sunday, we worshiped at an Orthodox church, which was a new and different kind of experience for both of us. Early on Monday morning, we began our long journey westward.

+ + +

Standing in our new living room, the foreman of the moving crew handed me a tablet. "Just press your thumb on the scanner port, Mr. Frazee." I did so. "It's been a pleasure working with you. If you find any damage, please let me know within a week."

I nodded. "Good, thank you, Tony." He turned and went out the door. I looked at Debra Sue. "What do you think?"

"It's even more beautiful...." As she started to answer, the doorbell rang. "Hold that thought!"

When she opened the door, John and Nancy were standing on the stoop. Nancy pointed towards the moving crew foreman getting into his truck. "They're all done already?"

I walked towards them. "Hey, you two, we won't be ready to go to dinner for at least another hour!" We all shook hands.

Nancy looked towards the ceiling. "This is incredible! You selected this based upon virtual reality tours and photos?"

Debra Sue nodded. "That's it. As I told Frank, my generation is used to dealing with virtual reality tours, but people in his and yours are not."

I pointed upward. "The beams in the open beam ceilings and all the corner posts are cedar logs. The clothes closets are lined with cedar paneling. Most of the paneling is natural redwood. The outside walls are insulated R-60, and the roof is insulated R-90. We have our own well, geothermal A/C, and solar power. My parents would have shaken their heads in near disbelief if they had seen this."

John nodded. "It sounds like this is even more up-to-date technologically than ours is, and that's saying something." He looked up and around. "This open-beam room seems full of space, and yet everything seems rather ... I guess 'cozy' is the word."

Nancy smiled. "Yes! It is cozy. I don't see any grills. How is this heated?"

I pointed toward the floor. The heat is in the floor. When we need A/C, there are outlets hidden in the rafters. With so much insulation, all this doesn't require much of either. There're no boxes on the sofa or love seat. Let's sit down."

Nancy handed Debra Sue a bottle of champagne. "I know that you two aren't really drinkers, but this is alcohol-free."

Debra Sue smiled. "I think we'll save it for a year from today, to celebrate our first anniversary here. We're going to be too busy to celebrate over the next few weeks."

During the next hour, Debra Sue and I told them about our farewell party at the Kansas City church, and about our journey to Oakland. My children and their families were in Kansas City for the farewell worship service and the party. We didn't do much sightseeing on our westward journey. John and Nancy had only a few questions before taking us out to dinner, where we answered a few more questions. After they dropped us off outside the motorhome, we practically collapsed into bed.

When I awakened the next morning, Debra Sue was nowhere to be seen. She left me a note.

> *Frank, let's read scriptures and worship after lunch.*
> *There's breakfast for you, ready to be re-heated, in the*
> *microwave. Fruit's on the table. Coffee's in the pot. I'm*
> *working on setting up our new kitchen. -- LOVE*

What a woman!

Later, when I was walking from the motorhome to the house, my phone rang. "Hello?" I paused in my walking.

"Pastor Frank, this is your architect, Leroy Wright."

"Good morning, Leroy, how are you?"

"I'm blessed far more than I deserve, Pastor Frank. After you and John Wells approved the plans I drew for the first three buildings, I've continued to work on an alternative set of plans. If you don't want to use them, I'll simply keep them on my computer and perhaps sell them elsewhere in the future. I want to show them to you, and if you like them, I'll show them to John."

I resumed walking towards the front door of the house. "Okay. Debra Sue is working in our new kitchen, unpacking boxes and setting things up the way she wants them. I'm going to be in my study if you want to come to the house."

"Okay, Pastor Frank, I'll see you in about thirty minutes." The call ended.

I let the retina scanner unlock the door, and I walked in. Like the virtual reality software, I was still getting used to the newest technology. I called out. "Good morning, my love!"

I heard her voice faintly respond. "Good morning" from the kitchen. When I walked in, she was arranging cookware. "You were sleeping so peacefully, I thought I'd let you sleep. Did you eat breakfast?" She turned and put her arms around me. We kissed deeply.

"I had plenty, thank you. I just got a call from Leroy Wright. He'll be here in a half-hour or so. He wants to show us some alternative plans to consider for the church."

"Really?"

I nodded and scowled. "I'm not sure I want even to consider alternatives, but I'm going to pray until he gets here."

"Okay. When he gets here, I'll get the door and show him to the study."

"Okay." I gave her a light kiss, turned, and went out. I arranged the study to keep it simple. The desk had a comfortable executive chair. Facing it on the other side were two overstuffed chairs. There were bookcases on three walls. Near the window behind my desk was my prie-dieu, which I had brought from my office in Kansas City. There were four more chairs stacked in a corner.

I knelt on my prie-dieu, and I was still praying when I heard the doorbell. I got up and greeted Leroy, just as he and Debra Sue got to the door.

"Good morning again, Leroy. Debra Sue, why don't you stay and look at these plans with me?"

As he unrolled large sheets of paper he took from a tube, he explained. "I did not bring the blue prints, which are already complete but not approved by the city. I just brought drawings depicting how the outside and inside it will look when complete. This plan puts the first three buildings under one roof. First, here's the side facing the street and the parking lot."

I was surprised, yet not quite as surprised as I could have been, had I not spent the previous half-hour in prayer. Debra Sue's mouth was hanging open, and she closed it momentarily before she pointed and spoke. "That looks like a log hotel about twice the size of that big one in Yosemite Valley. The walls aren't logs, though."

Leroy nodded. "Correct. The natural wood logs that are framing on the outside simply provide accents to the nearly earthquake-proof and heavily insulated overall structure. The worship area is in the center, with classrooms, offices, nursery, storage, and meeting rooms on the left, and with a commercial kitchen, more storage, and three dining and meeting rooms on the right. There're rest rooms along both sides. The worship area easily converts into the largest dining area. At current construction costs, it will cost slightly less than the plans you already approved. For earthquake stability, it will sit on pilings going to thirty feet underground, just as with the other plans." He opened another sheet of paper. "This is how it will look from down the hill from the west."

I nodded. I was beginning to feel a sense of peace and excitement. "Let's see the worship area."

The architect turned over two pages. It was beautiful. It was like the inside of a giant log cabin. Leroy pointed out the key points. "The log beams hide most of the technology we associate with worship. Between each of the hidden speakers throughout the sanctuary are microphones. The outputs from those microphones are fed into a computer that reduces noises and echoes. The video screen is 8K solid-state so that projectors aren't required, and lighting can be creative, just as it was in the previously approved plans."

I looked over the plans carefully, and Debra Sue stepped away to stare out the window behind my desk. Leroy stopped talking as I digested what I was seeing. "This design provides old-world beauty with modern comforts and innovations. It will be appealing to people of several generations." I paused. "I'm comfortable with this." I took out my phone and dialed a familiar number. "John? This is Frank."

"Pastor Frank! Good morning! What's up?"

"I'm here in my new office with Leroy. He's been showing Debra Sue and I," I paused to look at her, and she gave me a subtle wink, "some alternative plans for construction of our new church. We think you and Nancy should see them as well. I'd like the four of us to pray about this until after our first worship service. Then, we can talk about the future again over lunch."

The surprise was obvious in John's voice. "Wow, Frank, we all loved those other plans, so this is somewhat of a shock. What about our budget?"

"Leroy says it will perhaps cost us a little less."

"Really! Okay, tell Leroy I look forward to seeing them. We'll talk again later. Bye."

"Bye." We hung up. I looked at Leroy. "He was shocked, and I'm not surprised. He says he looks forward to seeing these plans, but I think he's a little upset about making this huge change after we got comfortable with the previous plans."

Leroy nodded. "You keep these copies. I've got other sets. I'll also email all of it to you, so you can compare feature for feature on your computer. Right now, though, I'll head over to see John and Nancy." We shook hands. He shook hands with Debra Sue, and then he rapidly walked out of my study.

My beloved looked at me. "The only bigger surprise in my life than this was our last conversation with Elyse. I wonder what she's thinking about this!" She smiled.

I nodded. "We've got a lot to think about and pray about. Right now, though, I've got all of this room to unpack."

"It will take me the rest of the day to get the kitchen organized. Tomorrow I want to work on our master bedroom, and I'll need your help with that."

I must have had a big smile. "Once we have our bedroom ready, we can start actually living in our new home!" She returned my smile and walked towards me.

+ + +

The day before Labor Day, as I called everyone to worship under the big tent, I was excited to look out over an ethnically-diverse sea of faces. Later, Debra Sue estimated that there were nearly three hundred there. Afterward, we greeted people. Two conversations stand out in my memories of that day.

An African-American couple approached us as worship concluded. He was linebacker-sized and in his twenties. She was slightly shorter. "Good morning, Rev. Frazee. I'm James Fields, and this is my fiancée, LaVonne." We shook hands.

"Good morning, we're glad you joined us. Do you live here in Oakland?"

They both smiled. LaVonne was effervescent. "We're so glad we came. We saw the ad in the paper last Sunday and had to stay through this morning. We grew up here in Oakland, but James has one more year at Fullbrite Seminary starting this week, and

I'm finishing my Master of Arts in Music at California College of Music. We'll be returning to Oakland next Spring and plan to get married and start a family."

James nodded. "After your closing prayer, LaVonne and I looked around at the people and looked at each other. We nodded simultaneously and smiled. To you, that does not mean anything, but LaVonne and I have known each other since we were small children. When we come back to Oakland next May, we'll get married, and we'll make this our church home. Right, LaVonne?"

She nodded enthusiastically. "Yes! I'm sure there's work for us to do here. There are others in his Fields family that are here today, as well as from my family. We also recognize Chinese and Hispanic families with whom we're acquainted."

Debra Sue smiled. "Wonderful!"

James also nodded. "That's not all! In my undergraduate days, I played football, and our team doctor and his wife are here. His name is Frank Pooler. He's Swedish, I think, and he's what people call a general practitioner."

I nodded. "I met him earlier. He's a friend of the man who secured the land for this church, John Wells."

James suddenly had a huge grin. "John Wells! I thought I saw him at a distance this morning. He helped my team get some special equipment for our gym." He looked around. "You've got other people to greet, so we'll move along, but we'll see you next May!"

LaVonne nodded. "Next May! Bye!" They moved on.

Debra Sue looked at me. "With him graduating from Fullbrite next May, one or both may end up being on our staff someday!"

I nodded. "That could be. That's more to pray about."

We greeted dozens of others, and then an Asian couple approached. I greeted them. "Good morning! I'm Pastor Frank Frazee, and this is my wife, Debra Sue."

They both smiled. "I'm David Eng, and this is my fiancée, Jennifer." We shook hands, and Jennifer and Debra Sue shook hands.

David spoke quietly. "I'm the only one in my family who follows Jesus. Jennifer would not go out with me unless I went to church with her on Sundays. At first, I was simply a spectator, but then I bought a CUV translation of the Bible with the simplified script, with NIV English. It's a Manadrin Chinese - English bilingual Bible, and Jennifer and I began reading it together. Once we started reading the Bible together, I could not stop, and I invited Jesus into my heart. I feel so very different. At her insistence, I have begun teaching her Mandarin Chinese. I am a general contractor. I heard you say that you are going to break ground here on this hill for a permanent structure. If you have not engaged a contractor, I would like to be considered."

I felt something deep within me, and I knew God was giving me a nudge. I smiled. "I think you're the man whom Debra Sue and I have been praying about. If you and Jennifer do not have any plans for lunch, would you like to join us, along with John and Nancy Wells, some friends of ours?"

David looked at Jennifer, and she nodded. "Of course! We'd love to join you. I am curious. Who is your architect?"

"Leroy Wright."

"Excellent! I was the general contractor when he and I built the New Hilton in Palo Alto a few years ago. He's an excellent architect." He paused. "Speaking of Leroy, there he is!" David pointed.

Leroy was talking with John and Nancy, and she saw David pointing. The three of them started walking towards us.

Seven of us had lunch together at the Burma Superstar on Telegraph Avenue, where we enjoyed Burmese cuisine.

6.

Growth and Construction

*We planned to hold our first worship service
in the new building on the Fourth of July,
but completion was delayed until
September. First, there were increasing
numbers of people, an earthquake, a brush
fire, and construction complications.
Furthermore, Debra Sue got pregnant.*

Two weeks later, after the worship service under the tent, we
broke ground officially for the church. A free-lance video
company recorded it all and put it out on the Internet, along with
the URL for the church's web page. In October, David Eng and
his crew began pouring concrete for the pilings. The second day,
Debra Sue and I were looking at the top of one of the pilings that
had been poured the previous day, when the ground began to
shake. Debra Sue looked at me. "Do you remember when that
man put a hole in my blouse?"

I nodded. "Let's stand here by the piling, holding hands."
We faced each other, on either side of the piling, holding hands.
We closed our eyes. "Master," I began, "we know there's power in
your name."

"Master," Debra Sue continued, "you promised that you
would do whatever your disciples asked."

"Yes, Master," I said, "You said you would do it, so that
Your Father would be glorified."

"Yes, Master," she said, "We now ask that you hear our
prayer, that God may be glorified."

"Master, may your will be done in a peace that endures, both
above the ground and in the ground. Amen."

"Amen."

Suddenly, the earthquake stopped, and everything was still. The ground was still. The air was still. There wasn't a sound of any kind.

We heard the crunch of gravel, as David Eng walked over to where we were standing around the piling. He was smiling. "All hail the power of Jesus' name! I don't know what you two prayed, but it worked! Praise God!"

Together, Debra Sue and I replied, "Praise God! Amen." We let each other's hands go, got together to one side of the piling, and hugged.

David took out his phone and pushed a few digits. He looked at the screen. "Look at this! This is the seismograph at Berkeley. It's now a straight line. No aftershocks!"

We looked. There wasn't a quiver. I started singing an old hymn, and Debra Sue joined me.

> All hail the power of Jesus' name,
> > let angels prostrate fall.
> Bring forth the royal diadem
> > and crown Him Lord of all!
> Bring forth the royal diadem
> > and crown Him Lord of all!

We hugged again. As we walked to our car, the workers resumed pouring the pilings. As we drove away, I was thoughtful regarding what had just happened. "I suspect that this won't be the last miracle that we see as we continue this new ministry."

She was quiet, then spoke softly. "Amen to that!"

Almost two months later, as November began on the first Sunday, the weather turned much colder. After a worship service that was briefer than usual because of the cold, and after the closing prayer, I spoke firmly. "I've shortened the worship service today because most of us are shivering. We warned everyone last month that when the weather got too bad that we would take down this tent and start worshiping in rented space. That time has come." I paused.

"At the bottom of the hill, there's the old shopping center that is being re-developed. We have rented the space that used to be a department store. It won't be turned into a theater until late next year. We need some volunteers this week, to help move everything under this tent, along with everything in the storage building in our parking area, down the hill to that old department store. If you can help, go to our web page. All the details will be posted there this afternoon. Get warm, everyone, and have a blessed week!"

The next morning, we did not start putting our breakfast dishes in the dishwasher until nearly 8:00. Debra Sue had a doctor's appointment at 8:30, so she was moving quickly. "You're on your own for lunch today, Frank. I'm having lunch with Jennifer and some of her Asian friends at Shan Dong Restaurant. She's been telling them about our church, and she wants me to tell them my story, from the time I was first hired in Kansas City."

I was pleased. "That's great!" I brought over some more dishes from the table. "I got an email yesterday from James Fields. He and LaVonne are coming up here mid-December, and they'd like to provide some special music for Christmas. I think that if one or both of them are going to be on our staff, it will be a good opportunity for more people to get to know them. They won't go back south to school until after New Year's."

Debra Sue hummed. "Maybe we should have a New Year's Watch Night Party."

I was startled. "That hadn't occurred to me! It wouldn't be hard to organize."

She nodded. "Right." She paused as she closed the dishwasher. "Ever since I saw the smoke coming up the hill three weeks ago because of that little brush fire, I've been wondering if we need to have some kind of protection down below the church building."

We started walking into the bedroom to finish getting ready to go. "I've thought about it too. We own the land all the way down to the boulevard. I'll talk to Leroy today. Maybe we should install sprinklers and some ground cover."

She was ready to go, and we stopped to kiss. "I'll be interested in what Leroy has to say. He probably knows a good landscape architect. I'll see you this afternoon. Jennifer is coming back with me and help me do some decorating. She has some interesting ideas."

"Okay, see you later!"

"Later!" She walked briskly to the door into the garage and was gone.

A few minutes later, I drove to the construction site. The tent was being struck, and trucks were loading up to move things to the old department store. John Wells was directing all the work.

I parked near where John was standing and got out. It wasn't raining, but the sky was dark, and there was a cold breeze coming from the ocean. "Good morning, John!"

He turned. "Good morning, Pastor Frank!" We shook hands. "Leroy has been talking to a landscape architect named Bobbi Ryan. I trust their judgment. They want your approval on some things she has planned. They're over there in the trailer office." He pointed.

"Okay." I walked the fifty yards or so briskly in order to stay warm. As I usually did, I opened the door and went inside without knocking.

Leroy was talking with a woman in her thirties. He turned to see me come in. "Good morning, Pastor Frank! I want you to meet Bobbi Ryan, our landscape architect."

I stepped forward and shook her hand. "It's a pleasure to meet you. Do you have a church home?"

"Yes, I belong to Central Broadway Baptist Church downtown. I've heard so much about you. It's nice to meet you too."

Leroy pointed at the easel where they were standing. "I showed Bobbi the land and the plans right after you and John approved them. She's worked up a tentative proposal for us. We need your input."

She pointed as she talked. "I made sure we could keep all the large trees that were already here, and Leroy has placed the building well away from their root systems." She pointed lower on the drawing. "I'm glad you're going for compacted concrete pavement for the parking lot. The environmental impact makes it easier for me to plan low-maintenance shrubs and perennials."

As she spoke, I looked at the overall layout, and I was curious. "Leroy, did you consider breaking up the parking slightly, and putting shrubs between the sections? We would have to supply simple irrigation for those beds, with the ability to replace pipes easily when necessary."

He nodded. "That's easy, and it's only a minor modification. I'll have a possibility or two by the end of the week."

I nodded. "All the of the rest of this looks good. I see you're providing for seasonal flowers in flowerbeds near the main entrance, Bobbi."

"Yes. They don't have to be seasonally planted, but I think you'll want some color there."

"I like that. What about the hillside below?"

She pulled out another drawing. "I think you should go for something that will require low maintenance, will endure, and be somewhat fire-resistant."

"Yes!" Leroy was emphatic. "She's suggesting is a new technology, and I like it. It is just as…. Bobbi, you can explain it better than I can."

She nodded. "Leroy had planned on 'rain-birds' regularly showering the hillside from the top. The problem with that might be water restrictions if there is a drought, or if the cost of water goes up significantly." She pulled out another drawing. "This is a sub-surface drip system. Even when the surface soil is dry, the soil six inches down and more remains moist. First, we'll remove a few inches of the hillside's topsoil. We'll install a newly-developed subsurface irrigation system, covered with about a foot of a moisture-holding mixture developed over at U.C. Davis, and cover that with the previously removed soil. We'll plant Yerba Buena or *Satureja douglasii* about every 18-inches. It thrives in the special mixture from U. C. Davis."

Leroy was enthusiastic. "If you approve, I think you'll love it. It will require little or no maintenance, and it will make the hillside below the church attractive."

"Debra Sue and I have been praying about this whole project for months. This all seems right. Bobbi, it seems to me that for those flower beds near the entrance and elsewhere, we can have different colors bloom at different times of the year, but all planted together, can't we? I've seen it done in arboretums."

She nodded. "I can certainly give it some more thought."

"Have you ever seen Butchart Gardens in Victoria, British Columbia?"

Bobbi's eyes got bigger. "I've certainly heard of them, and I've seen pictures and videos, of course."

I pointed. "I see a nice wedding set on your finger, so I think what I'm about to suggest will be worth it. If Debra Sue and I arrange for you and your husband to spend a week in Victoria, would you arrange to spend some time consulting with the groundskeepers of the gardens there and get some ideas from them? I hope they will not charge too much to consult with them. They might give you some ideas in addition to what you've presented here. We'll cover your air fare, a motel, and a stipend for meals. What do you say?"

Bobbi's mouth hung open. "Absolutely!"

"Great! Look at your calendar, discuss it with your husband, and get back to me."

That evening, Debra Sue and I celebrated another first over our dinner. She was pregnant. The nursery of the new building would get used right away.

+ + +

Several weeks passed. Leroy and I were standing in the middle of the sanctuary. It was cavernous! The floor was bare and unfinished. Only log beams interrupted the space between the floor and the ceiling high above. Temporary floodlights lit everything from below, creating strange shadows. High above us, electricians were installing the hidden lighting fixtures on top of the log beams, their voices being heard sporadically.

Leroy shook his head. "Pastor Frank, I've got a cockeyed feeling. It's almost like something isn't quite right, but I can't put my finger on it."

I looked at him. "There's an old story I remember about Dodger Stadium. No one noticed something until during the first game on opening day. The architects, Kroger-Savanah-Canterbury, had forgotten to put drinking fountains in the plans."

"You're kidding!" He burst out laughing. "That's sad, but it's a great reminder that the best architects can make mistakes because we're human. They were great architects!" He laughed again, looked around again, and then looked at me. "Is there anything at all that you'd do differently, or do you remember a church where the design was both traditional and innovative?"

I carefully looked around. "One image comes to mind, Leroy, but I don't know how useful it might be to you. It is not something I would have planned, but it worked."

"Shoot."

"Down in San Diego, there is a chapel that has less than a hundred feet from the rear doors to the stained glass above the altar. Like countless other churches, the floor is roughly in the shape of a cross, just like this building, only smaller, with the nave, the chancel, and two transepts."

"Okay."

"As you face the front, in the left transept, there's a large walk-through baptistery, where the chairs can be reversed for small and private baptisms. The only better baptistery I ever saw was just outside a glass wall in south Florida, where the pool had a waterfall and was surrounded by orchids. Here, we've got the baptistery at the rear of the chancel, much further from the congregation."

Leroy was thoughtful. "I'd not considered that possibility. I've just planned to put seating in the two transepts. In that little chapel, what about the other transept?"

"It had overstuffed furniture and space for wheelchairs. As you know, some churches have movable partitions or curtains to close off the transept areas. In Kansas City, we often put the coffin in a transept area during funerals."

Leroy nodded. "In an early version of this building, I had light shafts in the transept areas. It would be easy to add them back in." He was thoughtful. "Pastor Frank, you've given me another point of view. Let's talk tomorrow again. I'm sure you have pictures of your Kansas City church, but I wonder if the Internet can provide us with images of that chapel?"

I nodded, took out my phone, and touched a button. "Hey, gorgeous! Have we got enough for a few guests for lunch?"

"Sure! Why? How many?"

"Leroy is here, and I suspect he may want his new wife to join us." (Leroy suddenly had a surprised and smiling look.) "I haven't talked to John and Nancy today, have you?"

"They are joining us already. I talked to Nancy about a half-hour ago. Do you want to eat out?"

"No, Leroy and I need to dig through some of the pictures from Kansas City's sanctuary, and I need to search for pictures on the Internet of a chapel I've seen in San Diego."

"Are you talking about the church complex at the top of a hill on the north side of the city?"

"Right."

"Okay. That'll make six of us for lunch. I'll just set up a taco bar, with a fruit salad, soft drinks, and cookies."

I felt myself smile. "I love it when you get your creative juices flowing."

"Me too. Shall we say 12:30?"

"Sure! I love you!"

"I love you too!" We ended the call.

I turned to Leroy. "John, Nancy, and you – and your new wife if she's available, are invited to have tacos with us at 12:30. John told me yesterday that you and your long-time girlfriend eloped last weekend."

His face broke out with a big smile.

"Yes! Our families were disappointed they weren't there to see us, but they understood it was because of our tight schedules. She does interior designing for commercial buildings." He took out his phone and punched numbers. "Hi! We're invited to Pastor Frank's home for lunch. How about I pick you up in 45 minutes?"

His bride's voice was very animated. "This is great! I've been wanting to meet them. I'll be ready."

Leroy smiled. "Okay, see you later. I love you!"

"I love you too."

As Leroy put away his phone, I looked at my watch. "It's a little past 11:00 now. I have one further thought about something you and I have not discussed. As a church architect, you're familiar with those circulating baptistery heaters that are heavily promoted to churches and very popular."

"Right. I have one ordered for this church."

"I know from friendships with other pastors and my own experiences, that those things can let us down unexpectedly, and as they get older they can get noisy."

"Really! You're the first pastor that's said anything."

I nodded. "By nature, most of us are not complainers. Anyway, even if upgrading to a more reliable commercial setup costs us twice as much, please look at our options, will you?"

"These little details are easy to fix, Pastor Frank."

"Okay. I'll see you at lunch."

"See you later."

I left.

By the time our doorbell rang the second time with Leroy and his bride, I had printed out pictures from both Kansas City and San Diego. Leroy's bride, Angela, was almost as tall as I am, and Debra Sue and I could see that they were hopelessly in love.

After a very filling lunch, we went into the study. I laid out the pictures I had printed on my desk. John and Nancy were very familiar with the Kansas City pictures, of course, but they studied the ones from the chapel in San Diego and the Florida church carefully, as did Leroy and Angela.

Angela was particularly taken with the baptistery in Florida. "Leroy, as we were driving up here you said you were considering putting the light shafts back into the transepts, that would be ample light for orchids. Bobbi Ryan and I could help you design some planters with an automatic drip watering system, and we could even include a waterfall amidst the foliage."

"I think that would be great! What do the rest of you think?"

Debra Sue and Nancy were nodding. John was skeptical. "Wouldn't it require significant maintenance?"

I shook my head. "One of the reasons I like this is because the church in Florida never touches the orchid plants. They just let them grow, and once or twice a year they may trim runners that get too long. Orchids are low-maintenance if the planters are designed well."

Angela was nodding. "I'm sure Bobbi and I can work out all of that. Leroy, this will be another chance for us to work together, only this will be unique for us."

John nodded. "I'm sold. What about you, Pastor Frank?"

"I'm good with this part. Angela, I'm sure you can help Leroy with finishing touches in the Foyer, as well as the rest of the building. What about the other transept? It is a little large for just a sofa, a few chairs, and space for wheelchairs."

She was thoughtful. "If there are light shafts in both transepts, we could have an orchid garden on that side as well, maybe with a miniature waterfall. We'll have to make sure that neither waterfall produces much noise."

7.

Dedication and Beyond

During the nine months went by between the approval of the revised plans and the weekend the massive building was first used, my emotions went up and down, sometimes rapidly. Lettie called twice, saying she missed me, as our friendship was continuing, and I enjoyed those conversations. Malcolm and Paula Jeppley emailed us, saying they were taking a vacation in the area and would join us for our first Sunday. That was exciting. It would be his first month of not writing columns in the Kansas City newspaper in more than twenty years.

On the Friday morning before Labor Day, I was standing at the bottom of the steps leading up to the stage at the front of the sanctuary. With me were Debra Sue, Leroy and Angela Wright, and John and Nancy Wells. As I looked around, I was very pleased with what I saw. "Leroy, I'm glad you weren't satisfied with the original plans, because I know that this has turned out better than either Debra Sue or I had dreamed."

He smiled. "I'm glad you like it."

John nodded. "I agree. Before Frank and Debra Sue moved here, I thought they would be pleased with those plans, but I'm also glad we went for all of these natural wood posts and beams. It creates a warm and strong feel, even as you come in."

I had one concern. "As I recall, there was going to be a drinking fountain out in the foyer."

Leroy nodded. "I called the distributor yesterday, and he says that fountain and four others will be delivered today. Our plumbing contractor will be here this afternoon to install all five of them. They are refrigerated units, and the plumbing and electrical are already approved. It is simply a matter of hooking them up."

I nodded. "That's good. I doubt that tomorrow's wedding here will anywhere near fill the church. James and LaVonne say there was a total of just under 400 people that sent R.S.V.Ps." I looked at Debra Sue.

She smiled. "The florist will be here this evening to decorate. The reception they've planned can handle up to 500 comfortably. I've made it emphatic to the florist that everything except two sprays of flowers will have to be out of here when we lock up tomorrow night."

"Frank?"

I turned towards John.

"We'll have chairs for our honored guests for this Dedication Sunday over in the orchid garden transept. There will be room for three or four wheelchairs, just in case."

Angela was curious. "Who will the guests be?"

Nancy spoke excitedly. "We'll have State Senator Bahnmiller and his wife, Congresswoman Rita Fletcher and her husband, Mayor Luke Stark, and three Oakland City Council people. I don't know if all are bringing their spouses. Only Senator Bahnmiller and Mayor Stark will make any remarks as we dedicate the building."

I was pleased to, in my mind, "top" that. "For me, I think the best part of Sunday morning will be near the beginning, when I baptize nineteen people between some of the praise songs. I think I'm looking forward to that more than anything else. The youngest being baptized is a nine-year-old girl, and the oldest is a man in his sixties. We won't have our initial celebration of the Lord's supper here until the second Sunday. It would have made the service simply too long if we did it this first Sunday." Looking to the rear, I saw a uniformed police officer. "Excuse me," I said, "I see a familiar face. I'll be right back." The policeman and his wife had been with us from the first Sunday.

I went up the aisle, smiling. "Good morning Gary! You're in uniform, so you must be on duty. What's up?"

He took off his cap. "Good morning, Pastor Frank. I hope I'm not interrupting anything important."

I shook my head. "Not at all, Gary, today is probably the last day workers will be here, and we're sharing our final thoughts. What can I do for you?"

He smiled. "Nothing at all, Pastor Frank. My partner and I saw a few cars on the lot, and while he looks around outside, I came in to tell you a couple of things."

"Okay."

"I'm not on duty tomorrow, so I'll be here with my family. Some others in my precinct are bringing their families too, just to see the place now that it's finished and see what worship here is like. A couple of buddies and I are going to be keeping an eye out for any possible traffic problems, and if so, we'll take care of it."

I was stunned. "Wow! We weren't expecting police protection on our first Sunday!" I think I chuckled at that.

He shook his head. "Not really, Pastor Frank, it'll be nothing official. As you'll probably notice, the congregation is apparently going to include at least three police officers and their families, and I think there are going to be a few other first responders too. You and Debra Sue are among our most popular supporters."

Now I was amazed. "Really! I've simply made a few hospital calls, and I've stopped at the fire station and the police station at the bottom of the hill once or twice. We'll look forward to seeing you and your family on Sunday, Gary!"

"Thanks, Pastor Frank." He put his hat back on. "I'll see you Sunday." He strode across the foyer and out the double doors.

I turned and went back towards the front.

John looked concerned. "Are there problems?"

I shook my head. "As you know, there are first responders in our new congregation. That was Gary Thomason. He's coming with his family on Sunday, and a couple of his buddies are going to be here with their families. Gary and his buddies will be keeping an eye on traffic, just in case there are any problems."

Leroy's mouth was slightly open, and he closed it and cocked his head to one side. "As I was designing this campus, traffic problems were so far from my mind...."

Angela put her arm around him. "There's plenty of parking out there, isn't there?"

He nodded. "There's plenty of parking. This sanctuary is currently configured for twelve hundred. I've configured the framework for future expansion when or if needed."

Debra Sue and I were both surprised, and I think John and Nancy were too. I think my surprise must have shown in my voice. "Really! You're serious?" Everyone but Leroy looked stunned.

He nodded. "As you know, there are classrooms above the foyer and above the transepts. The light shafts are next to the doors into the classrooms. Those classroom spaces can be opened up to form balconies. By the way, there are partially hidden cameras in both transepts, so your baptisms can be depicted on the big screen, and your guests can simply stand where they are when they're introduced on Sunday." He looked at his watch. "Unless you've got other things you need to talk about, Angela and I need to go downtown for an appointment. We will see all of you on Sunday, okay?"

We said our farewells, and as Debra Sue and I walked towards the baptistery, John and Nancy excused themselves and went to the rear and out.

My beloved spoke quietly. "Let's see if the baptistery is starting to fill with water."

I shook my head. "It won't be filled until tomorrow afternoon. Did you know that the baptistery drain feeds into the hillside drip watering system?"

"Really! So, the water won't be wasted?"

"Nope. Is everything set for tomorrow's reception?"

"Oh yes, when Boots Clemson volunteered to be our wedding hostess, that was a load off my mind. She's going to be doing a great job, as you'll see at the rehearsal this evening."

+ + +

After Saturday's wedding, the guest count at the reception was 394. Debra Sue and I excused ourselves, and we went home even before the wedding cake was cut. After taking a shower, we got a good night's sleep.

The following morning, Dedication Sunday, I think I was more excited that day than any other day of my life. Looking out the window of the church's office, I could see that the parking lot was filling rapidly. I was dressed in cut-offs and flip-flops for the baptisms, but I had a change of clothes waiting in my private office.

As the praise team began the first of three songs, I spoke to a room full of baptismal candidates. "Good morning! I know some of you are nervous. Let me go over your routine one more time. When the praise team concludes the third song, I'll go down the stairs into the water and speak to the congregation for about two minutes. Then, Debra Sue will start one of you down the stairs, to join me in the water. Is anyone wearing flip-flops?"

There was a chorus of "No!" from a few of them.

"If you are wearing flip-flops, remember to leave them here in a place where you can identify your own. We don't want any of them to start floating on the surface, right?" They all nodded. "When you join me in the water, I'll ask you to tell the congregation why you want to get baptized today. When I put you under the water, pinch your nose with one hand. When you come up out of the water, I'll say a simple blessing, and you will go out the other side of the baptistery as the next person is coming down the stairs into the water. There are people waiting for you with towels, and they will take you to the dressing rooms where you put your dry clothing on. Does everyone understand?" They all nodded.

After the praise team finished leading the congregation in the third song, I started into the water, and everything went like clockwork. On the video screen, the sights and sounds were seen by everyone in the congregation. It took just over forty minutes to baptize seventeen people. Then the praise team led the congregation in three more songs. I changed my clothes.

Standing at the lectern I spoke about a few other activities during September and October, and then I told everyone to fill out the "Connection Card" each had been given at the beginning of the service. "Please be sure to include your preferred electronic mailing address, so we can keep you informed of what is happening in the life of the church. If you check the box indicating that you are joining the church today, please be sure to include your mailing address. Those joining between now and the end of October will be listed as charter members. Those we baptized today are registered as charter members already. Now, it's my privilege to introduce some special guests." I pointed to those seated in the transept opposite the baptistery, and the video screen displayed everyone in the transept. One by one, I introduced our special guests. The Mayor spoke about five minutes about the significance of this new church in a city with a rich history of churches both large and small. Then the Senator spoke about ten minutes about how, in a so-called "post-Christian Era," that the place for churches in each community are very important.

At the end of the service, after I said 'amen,' I went down the stairs to greet people, and Debra Sue joined me. I can still be terrible at remembering names, but, just like Elyse had, Debra Sue has near-perfect memory for connecting faces with names. She greeted those she knew as they approached.

"Good morning Mr. & Mrs. Fields!" We both smiled at them. "How soon are you leaving for the Oakland Airport and your honeymoon?"

Their smiles filled their faces. James shook my hand. "Our flight isn't until 4:00 PM. Thank you again for doing our wedding yesterday."

LaVonne hugged my beloved. "Thank you, Debra Sue! I know you did a lot behind the scenes to make our wedding so perfect!" She turned to me. "When we get back from our honeymoon, we will want to talk to you about joining the staff."

I smiled. "Wonderful! Debra Sue and I have already talked about that possibility. Have a great honeymoon! Where are you going, if I may ask?"

"Iceland!" They said it together and moved on, and the church's contractor and his wife approached. "Good morning, David, Jennifer!"

We greeted them, and as Jennifer shook my hand, she looked straight at me. "As you were baptizing about the tenth or eleventh person, a tall teenager, I whispered to David and told him I wanted us to transfer our membership up here to Hilltop Christian Center. He nodded in agreement."

Debra Sue shook his hand. "Wonderful! You two will be among our charter members. Have both of you been immersed in baptism?"

Jennifer smiled. "Yes! We won't have to be baptized again, will we?"

I shook my head. "No, as I said before the baptisms began, baptism is not about church membership. It is about following the example set by Jesus."

Debra Sue and I continued to greet people for more for a while before we left for lunch. As we were eating at the Brown Sugar Kitchen, she put her fork down to ask a question. "Have you and John decided on who is to be our church secretary?"

I chewed and swallowed some fried chicken before I answered. "Yes, definitely. He won't be anything like Lettie in Kansas City, that's for sure. Do you remember meeting Fred Webster after church about a month ago?"

She nodded. "I think so. Isn't he the semi-disabled fire chief?"

"Right. He'll be both Church Secretary and Business Manager. He'll take care of some of the administrivia I had to do in Kansas, so I'll have more time for ministry. Because of his background, he keeps his cool under all circumstances. As a younger adult, he was a police officer out in Marysville before getting firefighting training."

Our waitress approached. "Will you two be having some dessert? Today we have some vegan frozen chocolate dessert that is absolutely divine."

Debra Sue had a slight chocoholic smile. "I can't pass up anything chocolate! Did you say its vegan?"

"Yes, Ma'am, it is non-dairy. I'll have some here for you in a jiffy. What about you, sir?"

I nodded. "I'll have the same."

"Excellent!" She walked off quickly.

The dessert was truly delicious. When we left in the middle of the afternoon, we were both very full.

At the house, we went into our theater and started watching a streaming video news capsule. We wanted to watch a movie, but we couldn't agree on which of the latest ones we wanted to watch. After catching up on the news, we settled on an old science fiction classic called "Enemy Mine," with Dennis Quaid and Louis Gossett Jr. We were both surprised. Neither of us had ever seen it before, and it was thoroughly enjoyable. We added it to our list of favorites.

Monday morning, Fred Webster was already at work when I walked in at 8:30. "Good morning, Fred, you're here early!"

He nodded. "I've been an early riser since I was a teenager. I'm surprised to see you. I thought most clergy took Mondays off."

I shook my head. "I take the more traditional Sabbath. Unless there's a church activity that we must attend on Saturdays, Debra Sue and I make it a day of rest. Sometimes it's a day of prayer and fasting. Often, we leave town for the day. Are you getting settled in okay?"

"Sure! I've set up some directories on the church's computer, and I've just finished scanning yesterday's connection cards in. Counting the nineteen baptisms, we have four hundred seventy-eight charter members thus far out of a thousand forty-one connection cards filled out. There were a lot of people I didn't recognize."

"Wow! The sanctuary did look pretty full. We can't expect that many next Sunday. I'm sure there were some here as family support for those getting baptized, and some were simply curious about a new church."

"Right. I'm going to check our cyber security. Some of the baptisms, along with remarks by Mayor Stark and Senator Bahnmiller were on local news last night."

I nodded. "Debra Sue and I noticed that. We have a contract with Robinson Cyber Security. Give them a call."

Fred nodded. "Okay. I remember from yesterday you're starting a sermon series on love. Do you have anything specific for our electronic newsletter or our web page?"

"Sunday's message title will be 'Just One Love.' I'll upload a column later this morning or early tomorrow morning. This afternoon I'll be on the U.C. campus in Berkeley." I looked at my watch. "Put in a call to David Eng for me, will you?"

"Okay."

I went on into my office, and as I sat down, the phone rang. I looked up at Fred, who was nodding and pointing at his receiver. I picked up mine. "Good morning, David!"

"Good morning, Pastor Frank! We had a good crowd yesterday, didn't we?"

"Yes, David, a thousand forty-one connection cards were filled out. Last Friday, you mentioned being able to turn some of the classrooms into balconies. Can you briefly tell me about what that will involve?"

"I remember the surprised look on your face. Yes, if we remove the walls that separate those six classrooms from the sanctuary, we would have to put in risers of course, along with permanent seating up there. I've not developed the idea beyond that, so I can't tell you exactly how much it would increase the seating capacity. I can call Leroy to find out his vision for the area. I would guess, and this is only a guess, that we could add approximately six hundred to our current seating capacity. Since the floor is already engineered to support the weight, the construction would be fairly simple and straight forward."

"Thanks, David, I'll keep that in mind. Now that this project is complete, what's next for you?"

"I've already started on the restoration of an old Art-Deco theater in San Francisco. Jennifer and I are working together on that one. A restoration was attempted a long time ago, and then it was abandoned. The building is old, and it has become an eyesore. No one identified it as being in Art-Deco style until recently, and the historical society has gotten involved."

"Well, Debra Sue and I hope to see you and Jennifer once in a while. I know you're attending a church downtown."

"Let's plan on having lunch together soon, okay?"

"Okay, David. Bye!"

"Bye." We ended the connection, and I turned to my computer.

Down the hall, Debra Sue was looking at the entries Fred had made from the day before, trying to determine how soon she could start youth groups in addition to Church School classes.

74

8.

Temporary Leadership

*Why did I still dream of Elyse occasionally?
Now I was launching a church with Debra
Sue. As specified in the church's legal
charter, it would be a year before the
congregation could elect their leadership, so
we had to make many home visits during the
first two months. We had to determine who
among the charter members I would trust
and ask to serve for a one-year term of
temporary leadership.*

After the inaugural first worship service in the new building
on Labor Day weekend, the home visits seemed to go on endlessly
until just before Thanksgiving. John and Nancy Wells called on
as many people as Debra Sue and I did. Sometimes, instead of
visiting people in their homes, we would invite six or eight people
into our own homes. In addition, each week John and I invited
some men to breakfast or lunch, and on the same day Nancy and
Debra Sue would invite some women to lunch.

Debra Sue and I had John and Nancy over to our home for
Thanksgiving Day. Although Debra Sue roasted a turkey and
fixed several other things, John and Nancy brought over some
contributions to share as well. After I prayed, first we ate silently,
except for compliments on the food. There was a lot on my mind.
"I think my records are pretty well up to date. Of the six hundred
eighty-nine charter members, we've had at least three
conversations with all but seven of them, with whom we've had
two conversations."

Nancy sipped some coffee. "Let's wait until the day after
Christmas to start picking out temporary leaders."

We looked around at each other and nodded. Debra Sue passed the cranberry sauce to me as she responded. "Yes, I hope you can announce the temporary leaders you've appointed under the charter as pastor by the end of January. I'm not due until after Easter, but we need to start doing business as a chartered non-profit long before then, don't we?"

Again, there were nods around the table, as John reached for more turkey and spoke. "Our offering's income has made us self-sustaining since our second month under the tent, and soon our average attendance will be reaching the attendance of Dedication Sunday. Do you plan on launching a second service after the first of the year?"

I remember putting my fork down at that moment. "When Debra Sue and I had left Kansas City, we did not envision having more than one service for at least three to four years. It has been only fifteen months since we held our first worship service in the tent. I didn't even think about it until Dedication Sunday, when I looked out over the crowd. Since then, I've thought about it nearly every day."

Debra Sue stopped eating as well. "I think we need to continue to have church school on Sunday mornings at the same time. As with Kansas City, I'm at least temporarily Director of Christian Education."

Nancy nodded. "Yes, but don't we need to start Bible study groups for those thirteen and older?"

We talked about studies for men, for women, and for teens. We also discussed special-interest workshops. After dessert, we began discussing the role of Hilltop Christian Center in the larger Oakland Community, and how we need to do an in-depth survey of the community's needs. The discussion went on for several hours, and I can't begin to remember all of what we said.

It was after 11:00 when, as we were going towards the front door to say our good-nights, I asked if anyone knew when James and LaVonne were going to be ready to join the staff. Nancy nodded. "LaVonne told me last Sunday that she and James plan to make an appointment with you this coming week."

John nodded. "Our income is also sufficient to hire a custodian instead of using that service based in Orinda. James can easily be offered a decent package as a full-time Associate, and

LaVonne is ready to tackle being Minister of Music. We can talk tomorrow about whether or not to put the youth in James' portfolio or hire some part-time help. Last Tuesday night we had thirty high school kids and more than twenty middle school kids. Anyway, tomorrow is another day."

Debra Sue opened the door. "Okay, we'll see you tomorrow morning. Frank and I will be out of town most of Saturday, unless there's an emergency."

We said our good nights, but little did we know.

Just over four hours later, Debra Sue awakened me. "Frank! Frank!"

Suddenly, I was wide awake. I knew something was wrong from her voice. "What? What's going on?"

"My gut is killing me! I think you'd better take me to Kaiser Oakland."

That was all I needed to hear. She's not a complainer and generally very healthy and strong. We quickly dressed, got into my car, and headed down the hill. I drove to the emergency entrance, and because she had called ahead, there was a nurse with a wheelchair waiting for us. As they went inside, I parked the car. I was out of breath when I went in. A doctor was already examining her. She was saying, "Since you're pregnant, we'll do an ultrasound first."

Immediately I knew. I called John and Nancy, and they came down to join me in my vigil. The rest of the night and into the morning, everything was a blur. She miscarried. John and Nancy began calling several of the most active members, so prayer support began. Debra Sue did not check out of the hospital until Saturday afternoon. Even as this is written, we don't remember much of that weekend.

I began to compartmentalize everything. At home, I focused upon Debra Sue and didn't talk about what was going on at the church, unless she brought it up. Outside of the house, I had to put those concerns aside to focus on the church, but it was hard.

After church on Sunday, I told James Fields that I was hiring him as a full-time Associate Minister. I told LaVonne she would be Minister of Music. She had said she wanted to be on the Praise Team but not be the lead singer, and I agreed. I showed them their offices, gave them master keys, and gave them temporary passwords for their directories in the church's computer. We agreed to meet on Friday for planning and brainstorming.

On Monday, Fred Webster took it all in stride. His military and first-responder experiences made him able to rise above everything and focus on what needed to be done. From that day on, he became the church's extension of me. After I told Fred about the miscarriage, church issues I would have discussed with Debra Sue that day I discussed with Fred. I was (and still am) convinced that God had connected Fred to us when we needed each other. As I told Fred about my previous day's conversations with James and LaVonne, he took notes and suggested possibilities. He was happy to be useful, and I was happy with his help.

About midway through Monday morning, there was a quiet knock on the outer door of my office, and Debra Sue walked in. I stood up, and we held each other for a while. "I couldn't stay home and do nothing, Frank. I couldn't just mope about the house, letting my mind go in a hundred directions. I've got to work. Christian education programs always need leadership."

"Okay. Yesterday I hired James and LaVonne. I've given them their offices and keys. We're going to have a staff meeting on Friday and do some brainstorming."

She nodded. "Good." She paused, thinking. "As the Associate Minister, I think James can help me over the next few weeks with planning for the programming expansions we discussed with Nancy and John over dinner last Thursday. You never did share your thoughts that day about a second worship service."

I nodded. "I'm leaning towards either Wednesday evening or Friday evening. What do you think?"

She half smiled. "I'm still your traditional girl. I'm all for a mid-week service."

I smiled. "That's my preference too. I'm glad you and I agree on that. Let's shoot for the first Wednesday in February, okay? I've already decided upon having separate men's and women's Bible studies in homes, as soon as we establish some suitable leaders. We'll do a congregation-wide mixed adults Bible study each year after Easter."

Debra Sue nodded. "You and I have talked about that during pillow talk." She paused. "Okay, I've got things to focus upon for this morning."

"Good! Would you be interested in taking the BART over to the Westfield Center for lunch and some Christmas shopping?"

Again, she half-smiled. "Good idea! I can focus on Christmas for a while!" She turned, and she went out through the church office, stopping to visit quietly with Fred before going on out.

+ + +

Everyone we knew was very busy for the next month as we approached Christmas. On Christmas Eve, we had services at 5:00 PM and 7:00 PM. In the foyer between the services, we served coffee, tea, and hot mulled cider with cookies. Total attendance for the two services reached just over eighteen hundred. James helped lead the worship, and LaVonne was on the Praise Team, after she had worked out what music we would use.

At home, Debra Sue and I ate chicken tenders, snacks and ice cream while watching classic movies. We did not turn off the lights until after midnight. Christmas morning, we did not set an alarm, so instead of our typical scripture readings and prayers starting at 5:00 AM, we didn't start until nearly 7:00. Our prayers went on for more than an hour.

Before getting up, we talked. She spoke quietly and confidently. "Frank, I want us to keep trying to have a baby. I think I decided that as I sat down after reading Luke's account of Christ's birth during the first service."

"Debra Sue, you know I'm up for doing whatever it takes to get you pregnant!" We tickled one another and kissed for a while before getting up and getting dressed. I was glad that she was effectively moving on after our miscarriage.

By the time we reached New Years' Day, we were working hard at the church, preparing for a leadership dinner the following evening. I arranged for this dinner to be catered, so that everyone could focus on one another, and so that conversations could center around getting to know one another better and looking forward to the coming year.

The dinner itself went smoothly. After we had time to enjoy some dessert, I stood to speak. "As most of you have noticed, there are video cameras set up around the hall. Debra Sue and I want to have a historical record of this meeting. I'll now switch the video monitors around the hall from showing what the cameras are seeing to tonight's business." I touched a button on my phone. "Copies of everything I'll be showing you will be in your email."

As I talked, the displays changed. "First, here's a list of the church staff. Some of you have met Fred Webster, our Church Secretary. Raise a hand and wave, Fred!" He did so. "After our first month in this building, we switched from a custodial service to employing a member of the church. Grandy Papadopoulos is standing over there by the door." He waved.

"As most of you know, I have hired James Fields as Associate Minister, and I've hired his wife, LaVonne Fields, to be our Minister of Music. Originally, we planned for LaVonne to be part-time until we expanded our programming. That fact is already upon us, so she and James are both full-time. Their job descriptions will be in your email, along with job descriptions for Fred and Grandy.

"Our church's charter, registered with the State of California, provides for my appointing church leaders to serve for a year, followed by election of church officers. Our first election will be held the second Sunday of December, later this year. As I describe who I'm appointing for these temporary positions, remember that these positions are temporary for this first year in the building. Then we'll hold an election, and the congregation will take control of our leadership makeup."

I continued with the presentation until I had mentioned everyone in the hall. Then, I changed the focus. "All of you saw the crowds we had on Christmas Eve. Debra Sue and I are both amazed and praising God. After just over a year of existence on this hill, first under the tent, we are adding staff as well as expanding our presence within the community. It's very important that all of you remember what I'm about to say." I paused and drank a sip of water. "We must assume, *assume,* that we are going to have growing pains because of our rapid growth. After all, we have been in existence as a congregation for just over a year. There will be people who don't like things and stop coming. The Elders will call on them, listen to their concerns, and perhaps help them find another church home. There will be people complain about one thing or another, and most of it will be communicated through the church office. Right, Fred?"

Louder than was necessary, he called out "Right!"

There was quiet murmuring. "It is better to expect such things, and be possibly disappointed, than to be surprised. When my first wife, Elyse, and I first arrived in Kansas City, the average worship attendance was less than fifty. Today, the attendance in that church hovers in the range of two thousand. Over the quarter-century I was the pastor there, we had growing pains from time to time. Expect them, everyone!" I took another swallow of water.

"Labor Day has become our anniversary Sunday. We had our first worship under the tent on a Labor Day weekend, and our first worship in this building was on Labor Day weekend. By next September, some of you will be wanting to do something different after a year is up, and some of you will want to remain in your current positions. This is also provided for in our charter, a copy of which will be in your email. This too is expected. As I said earlier, our election will be held the second Sunday in December, and people will officially begin to hold their positions on the first day of the new year. Is that clear to everyone?"

There were murmurs and nods throughout the hall. I continued my presentation, talking about changes in programming. Later, as we got home and went in our front door, I said, "It's about time we start taking advantage of our pollution controls. I'm going to build a fire in our fireplace!"

Debra Sue grinned. "Great! I'll fix some popcorn!"

We sat in front of the fireplace, munching popcorn and talking about whatever came to mind. "I think that since this is James' first full-time call, he's a bit overwhelmed."

I nodded. "Yes.... There's a big difference between student churches and theories discussed in classes and engaging in the real thing on a large scale. He and LaVonne are going to have growing pains of their own. When she gets pregnant, they'll have more challenges. Speaking of which, when is your next checkup with your gynecologist?"

She swallowed some soda. "It's in two weeks...." She paused. "Do you hear sirens?"

I stopped to listen. "Yes! Video on! Local news!" The monitor above the fireplace lit up, and it displayed first responders surrounding an apartment house in flames.

"That's the apartment house on Redwood Road where Jim and Maxine Haddison live!" Debra Sue stood up to look at the display directly.

I took out my phone. "The Oakland Red Cross." It took almost a minute to get a connection.

"Oakland Red Cross, this is Polly. How may I help you?"

"This is Frank Frazee of Hilltop Christian Center."

"Pastor Frank! This is Polly Franz!"

"Hi Polly. Debra Sue and I are looking at our video screen and seeing the apartment house fire that just started. I think our Hilltop Christian Center is probably the closest approved shelter on your list. We can take everybody."

"Okay, I see on our file that I'm to call Fred Webster."

"That's right, Polly. Call Fred, and he'll take care of the rest. Are you going to get some sleep tonight?"

"Not until I go home, Pastor Frank. Bill is picking me up at 6:00."

"Okay, Polly, be blessed, and we'll see you next Sunday."

"Not next Sunday, Pastor Frank, Bill and I are going to Sequoia for a week."

"Okay, then we'll see you when we see you. Good night, Polly." We ended the call. Debra Sue was looking at me. "Polly Franz is on duty tonight at the Red Cross. She and Bill are going to Sequoia, so we'll see them in two weeks."

Debra Sue nodded. "When we start the home Bible studies, I think she and Bill will be good leaders."

"So do I. Right now, Fred will get the wheels turning at the church quickly enough. Let's plan on going in early and greeting people as they have breakfast."

"Good idea! Let's head for bed."

As an emergency shelter, the church was and still is ideal. It was simple to partition off the dining halls and kitchen from the rest of the church. Most of the people were placed in new housing in less than two weeks. Some of them started attending worship services, and two families later joined the church.

9.

Community Roles

The years rolled by quickly. Too soon, I would look at a special anniversary, when I would be married longer to Debra Sue than I had been married to Elyse. God blessed us in so many ways, but not with children. Debra Sue seemed to take it in stride, but I knew that she continued to hurt inside.

"Frank, our miscarriages have resulted in many hours of prayer. God has blessed us in innumerable ways, but I've concluded that we won't have children. Shall I make it certain in me, or do you want to take care of it?"

We were finishing our coffee after breakfast. Until that moment, it seemed like another typical day. I gazed at her steadily. "Dr. Klein can do it for me in his office. That's the simplest way."

"You don't seem surprised. Were you expecting me to say this?"

"I wasn't certain, but I wanted it to be your decision. I'm simply standing by your decision. Between nightly pillow talk, praying with each other, and praying for each other, we've become of one mind in so many parts of our lives. A vasectomy is an easy decision for me."

"Okay, if you're as sure as I am."

I took out my phone. "Dr. Klein."

The phone connected me quickly. "Oakland Urology Clinic. This is Sandra. How may I help you?"

"Sandra, this is Frank Frazee."

"Good morning Dr. Frazee. Do you need an appointment?"

"Yes, I need to get a vasectomy."

There was a pause. "Would Thursday afternoon at 2:00 be good for you?"

"Yes, that will be good. I'll be there."

"Thank you." We ended the call. "I'll see him Thursday afternoon at 2:00."

My phone rang, and I looked at the screen again. "It's Mike Panzer at the Board of Education." I touched the speaker button. "Good morning, Mike. We haven't talked in a while. What's up?" I put my phone on speaker.

"Good morning, Pastor Frank. You may have seen in the news that Ken Ray's funeral was last Friday. He served on the Board of Education for seventeen years. The Board has authorized me to appoint someone to fill out his last term, which is three and a half more years. Would you be willing to serve in his place?"

I looked over at my beloved, and she smiled and shrugged. "Mike, my wife and I pray about everything. Can I give you an answer tomorrow morning?"

There was a pause. "I wasn't expecting you to have to pray about it. Can you give me an answer before noon tomorrow?"

"Sure, Mike, but I will probably call you back about this time tomorrow."

"That's great! We'll talk tomorrow. Until then."

"Until then." I looked across the table as I ended the call. "When we get to the church, let's go into the sanctuary and pray about this before we go to our offices."

She nodded. "That'll be good."

"I'll put the dishes in the dishwasher while you finish getting ready, okay?" We both got up, and she headed for our bedroom.

About fifteen minutes later, we were kneeling at the rail at the front of the sanctuary. Since breakfast, my mind had been churning furiously, thinking about the obligations that might be required – including time – if I accepted this position. "Master, please allow us some time to know your presence before we talk with you about this." We were silent for several minutes. "Master, since the church is still going through growing pains, and because we're wanting to be more involved in the community, I have mixed feelings about this."

When I paused, Debra Sue cleared her throat. "Lord, I know Frank can do this and do it well, but I for one would like to have a clear sense of your will in this."

We both prayed silently for several minutes, and then we heard a door quietly open at the rear. I whispered. "For some reason, deep-down I think this just might be our answer."

We both got up, turned, and walked towards the rear of the sanctuary. Standing there by the door was a young mother. I recognized her. "Good morning, Pauline, how are you?"

When we reached her, both of us shook hands with her. She spoke quietly. "As you know, my son, Bobbie, is autistic, and he's still being bullied at school. I've talked to the principal, but I'm not at all sure that he's doing enough to help Bobbie."

I glanced at Debra Sue, nodding. "This is our answer." I looked back at Pauline. "Let's go to the office."

Debra Sue put her hand on Pauline's shoulder. "Everything's going to be all right, Pauline – I'm sure of it. Right now, I've got work to do, but I'll call you this evening." She went towards her office.

As Pauline and I went into the church office, Fred looked up. "Good morning, Pauline, Pastor Frank."

"Good morning, Fred. Pauline's autistic son, Bobbie, goes to Disney Middle School. Do you know the Principal there?"

Fred nodded. "His name is Richard Bettis. I've known him for years."

"What can you tell me about him?"

Fred was thoughtful. "Richard consistently has high expectations of students. He tries to be sure that disadvantages are not a barrier to the students' achievements. In that sense, I'm sure he cares about Bobbie's success despite Bobbie's autism. He's very supportive of the teachers as well."

"Before I talk to the principal, I want you to put in a call for me to Mike Panzer at the Board of Education." Fred turned away to start making the call. "Pauline, come on into my office." As we walked in, I closed the door. "Make yourself comfortable."

She sat down, and I went behind my desk. There was a soft chime. "Yes, Fred?"

"Mike Panzer is on line one."

"Thanks, Fred." I touched a button as I picked up the handset. "Good morning again, Mike. Debra Sue and I have prayed about it, and I will accept your offer."

"Excellent! I wasn't expecting this so soon."

"A problem has been brought to my attention, and I've got a parent sitting here in my office."

"Oh?"

"Have there been any problems concerning discipline in the last year or two at Disney Middle School?"

There was silence from Mike for several seconds. "I won't ask you about who is in your office right now."

"Good. If you'll talk, I'll listen."

"Okay. Two weeks before Ken Ray died, he led a rather vigorous discussion about discipline issues at Disney school. As you probably know, Richard Bettis is the Principal there, and, generally speaking, he is a pretty good administrator. In the past year or two, however, there have been discipline problems that have not been adequately addressed. I think Richard has a very good record, but because of family issues with him, I think he's not been adequately focused. I've spoken with him several times. I suspect that it is one of two issues. Is it about bullying, or is it about a teacher?"

"The former."

"Okay, then is it about an autistic boy named Bobbie?"

"That is correct."

"Very well. This is something I can address this morning. I'll head over there. The next Board meeting is a week from tomorrow at 9:00 AM. Meetings usually last the whole morning, but they seldom spill into the afternoon. Will that fit your schedule?"

I looked at my computer screen. "I'll be there. I'll see you then."

"See you then."

I turned to Pauline. "That was Mike Panzer, who, in case you don't know, is Chairman of the Board of Education."

Pauline's eyes got wider. "Really!"

I nodded. "He called me this morning just as Debra Sue and I were finishing breakfast. A long-time member of the Board died last week, and I've agreed to fill out his term. That means you're looking at a man who suddenly has some clout he did not anticipate having!"

"Wow!"

"'Wow' is right! Mike Panzer did not tell me what he's planning, but he's on his way over to your son's school. I'll call him back later to find out what transpired. Meanwhile, we can both hope that your son will not have to deal with that bully again."

A tear was running down Pauline's cheek. "Thank you, Pastor Frank!" She stood up, and she hugged me. I think she and I both sighed before she spoke again. "I'll let you know about whatever happens today after I talk to Bobbie this afternoon."

+ + +

My getting on the Board of Education was a turning point in those early years of the church. With all of my years of experience as a pastor, I was comfortable with everything as it unfolded. I had others on the Board join me as we held regular town-hall meetings with parents in the church, where they talked about various issues in the schools of their children. The meetings were strictly business, with the church acting simply as a meeting place. I functioned as Board of Education member and host but not as a pastor. The meetings included discussions about issues such as home schooling, charter schools, special education, and scholarships for education beyond high school.

After a few years, we started a scholarship program to pay for both trade school education and college education. We developed a fund for these efforts, but we also help publicize special scholarships sponsored by various businesses in the Bay Area. I neglected to make entries in my journal for a number of years because of the church's rapid growth.

As I had with Elyse, Debra Sue and I began taking summer-long sabbatical breaks every seven years. Those breaks kept us fresh, and I used part of the time to pray and prepare for a sermon series or two in the future.

Shortly after Debra Sue and I celebrated our twenty-fourth anniversary, the Elders of the church began talking about making a big deal of the church's silver anniversary, which was more than a year away. Matt Harris was enthusiastic. "It looks like we'll need to do three services this year on Christmas Eve. We're regularly filling all three balconies on Sunday mornings. Pastor Frank, have you thought any more about adding a third service?"

I nodded. "Yes, I've talked with James and LaVonne about it several times. I'm going to ask James to preach at least one service every Sunday, starting in December. That would be a good time to launch an early Sunday morning service. Furthermore, I think next year should be my last year of preaching every Sunday. Next summer, I'll start tapering off my schedule. We've been broadcasting our services live as well as on our web page for over a year. I think it is time to hire another associate minister. What do the rest of you think?"

That started a lively discussion that lasted nearly a half hour. Finally, Matt was thoughtful. "I think that you should be the preacher for our live broadcasts for a while."

I nodded. "I can do that, but starting next Summer, I'm going to be adding a full continuous month of vacation each year. I'm already taking four Sundays, scattered throughout the year, but starting next year I'm going to be adding to the number of vacation Sundays and reducing my salary package. We can start talking about that in January. Let's face it, I've been preaching for a half century now. I'm approaching eighty, and I'm going to have to retire eventually, unless you're expecting me to graduate into heaven while I'm still working."

That started another vigorous discussion.

+ + +

The final year of my being the full-time pastor, I encouraged the elders to help me find and hire another associate, who was to have primary emphasis on preaching. Others on the staff were not interested in being gradually phased in as the senior pastor.

The search took a practical approach. We sent out letters to seminaries all over North America posing a simple question: "Who are the ten best Christ-centered preachers whom you have heard, and with whom you are familiar?" The resulting lists we received varied widely, supplying us with a list totaling 93 men and 71 women. Debra Sue was particularly pleased with how many women's names appeared in the survey. There were three men's names and one woman's name who appeared on 91% of the lists. After Debra Sue and I discussed the results with the elders one evening, the following morning I made a phone call from my office to Robert Aki at his business. He was one of our charter members and a leader in Oakland's Asian community. We had first met Robert during the first month we worshiped under the tent. Debra Sue and I both liked him.

"Good morning, Aki Human Resources, how may I direct your call?"

"Good morning, this is Frank Frazee, may I please speak to Robert Aki? I'm his pastor."

"Just a moment please, Pastor Frank." There were a few seconds of silence.

"Good morning, Pastor Frank, I've been expecting your call. I understand that you and the elders have narrowed down your list."

"Good morning Robert. Yes, the lists we received varied widely. After we talk, I'll be sending you the information we have on 93 men and 71 women. Fred will get copies of all the correspondence to you later today or tomorrow. You should have them tomorrow morning at the latest. Three men and one woman appeared on most of the lists. From previous conversations with you, I understand that you have three on your staff that are both very capable and solidly Christ-centered."

"That's right. I have two women and one man who fit those parameters, and they will form a team to work with me to narrow down the choices. I know what kind of person the church is looking for. Those four that appear on most of the lists may or may not be among our final recommendations."

As Robert spoke, Fred came into my office and put a message on my desk. After glancing at it, I set it aside and took a sip of coffee. "Can you give me a rough idea of how you will proceed?"

"Sure, Pastor Frank, it's very straight forward. We will gather additional information on each of the people without approaching any of them directly. That will help us narrow down the choices. We will talk to people who know them, creating profiles of each person on the initially narrowed list. Every search is different, but since we're looking for leadership and preaching abilities, we'll examine video files on the final few before recommending a half-dozen or so to you. Then, as planned, they can be invited to preach here in Oakland on a Sunday when you are not preaching, and you and the Elders can meet with each of them."

I was surprised at how comfortable I felt with the process as he described it. Ending the call, I got up from my desk and opened Fred's door. "I'll be in the sanctuary for a while."

"Okay."

Going into the sanctuary, it was comfortably warm. I went about half-way down the center aisle before choosing a row of seats. After I sat down, I spent some quiet time, allowing myself to be present to God's presence. Gazing at the cross suspended over the chancel, I silently reviewed the previous evening's meeting and my conversation with Robert that morning. I examined the challenge from several different points of view besides my own. I wanted the transition to new leadership to go as smoothly as possible. In more than a half-century of pastoral leadership, I knew of many possible pitfalls.

I didn't know how much time transpired before Debra Sue sat down beside me. We looked at one another, and she put her hand on mine. "I assume you've called Robert."

I nodded. "Yes. I can tell you about the process later, if you like. Fred will deliver copies of all the correspondence to Robert's office probably sometime today."

"What do you think the timing will be like?"

"Robert did not commit to a time frame, and he told me that every search is different. Sitting here, discussing it with Our Master, I think our new Associate Preaching Pastor will be in place by late June, and on September's anniversary Sunday, I'll be announcing our trip to New Zealand, with the new Associate taking the full preaching and leadership load while we're gone. You've talked about going down under to New Zealand for years, and I think we'll stay in that part of the planet through November. What do you think?"

When I mentioned our going to New Zealand, a smile spread across her face. "This will be great! My new medium-format camera will make great videos and stills for us to share when we get back. We can share our hobby to the fullest. I'll post things on my page of the church's website as we go!"

I looked at my watch. "I've been praying in here longer than I thought. Do you think it's too early for lunch?"

"We'll make it brunch. I'm hungry!" When we stood, she took my hand. On our way out, I stopped and told Fred we were leaving. We had a wonderful brunch at P & J's.

The months flew by. The first candidate to take our pulpit for a Sunday appeared very qualified both on paper and in telephone interviews. We took him out to dinner after church, and that evening the Elders came to our house for a dessert meeting. The consensus was that he was not sufficiently seasoned with experience. Though he might have served very well, we thought it might be risky.

Seven weeks later, our candidate was a woman from a large church in Massachusetts. She abundantly met the qualifications we are seeking. However, she seemed uncomfortable with our particular ethnic mix. Two weeks later, our man was a candidate from Houston, Texas. We liked him, and he seemed to like us. After discussing all of our positive impressions, Debra Sue mentioned something the rest of us had overlooked. She attended these candidacy meetings because she knew the church and its people better than some of the Elders did. "Did any of you notice how two of the illustrations he used towards the end of his sermon sounded like they grew out of prosperity gospel thinking?"

Three of the Elders nodded. John Wells, now in his early nineties, had a surprised look on his face and cleared his throat before speaking. "Debra Sue, thank you. I couldn't put my finger on it until now, but you're right. I was uncomfortable with his story about the homeless woman from Austin. As a native of Houston, he's been exposed to prosperity gospel preachers from that area all of his life. If he leans in that direction, he would not be good for our church long-term. Pastor Frank has consistently preached what the Bible actually says, without much spin, and we need someone who can continue in that kind of preaching."

Over the next three months, we had two more candidates, but we were even less satisfied with what we saw and heard. Some of the Elders were getting discouraged. I was not. "I've been praying about this since I first asked Robert Aki to help us with the search. I told Debra Sue late last summer that I thought we would have our new associate in place by June. It's now mid-April, and Easter was three weeks ago. Who is scheduled as our next candidate, Chuck?"

Chuck Kamp was a psychiatrist and gifted counselor. "The next person on our list is a man named Elmer Hanson. He's been away from the pastoral ministry for over ten years because he's been teaching New Testament and preaching classes at Fullbrite seminary. When I last talked to him on the phone, he told me he misses pastoral ministry and as he put it, he wants 'to get back in harness.' Before joining the Fullbrite faculty nearly eleven years ago, he was the teaching pastor for Foothills Baptist Church, about a hundred miles south of here."

As I nodded, John Wells' face lit up. "I remember him! Nancy and I visited that church about fifteen years ago. He's a phenomenal preacher!"

That brought back memories for me as well. "I remember his teaching a seminar down at Asilomar. I liked him. Chuck, let's get him up here as soon as we can."

He nodded. "Right."

Three weeks later, when I greeted him at my office and shook his hand, I knew that Elmer was the man God had prepared for us. I also knew that God had been preparing the congregation for Elmer's leadership. Debra Sue immediately bonded with Elmer's wife, Ethelene. Hiring Elmer was a "no-brainer."

Over the July 4th weekend, I preached the televised via Internet service, and Elmer did the others. After church, Elmer, Ethelene, Debra Sue, and I had lunch together at the Brown Sugar Kitchen, which was a favorite for all of us.

All of us were very relaxed as we ate. We shared memories of our honeymoons and early years as couples. Then Elmer said, "This church is a life-changing experience for Ethelene and I. I don't know how else to put it."

Ethelene put down her fork, shaking her head. "I think that says it, Elmer, but it doesn't say enough." She looked at Debra Sue. "You're the big sister I never had, Debra Sue. I have a younger brother, Ethan, but I wish I had met you twenty years ago." She looked at me. "Frank, my Dad died when I was three. I don't have any memories of my Dad, and my Mom didn't re-marry until I was in college. I'd like to think that my Dad was like you."

My face must have turned red. "Ethelene, I do believe that's the nicest compliment anyone has ever given me!"

Debra Sue nodded. "Amen!"

Elmer was nodding, but his face was more serious. "We've bonded as friends more quickly than we might have expected, but what God is doing in this church overwhelms all of that. Look at the amazing growth of this congregation and the ministries it does for the community!" He drank a swallow of water. "Ethelene and I have talked about this. From the beginning, this faith community and the larger community have felt like a perfect fit for us. It's something only God could have accomplished."

Debra Sue and I expressed our full agreement. As difficult as the search had been, it had all been worth it. After preaching for one service each Sunday in June, he began preaching most services in July. I continued to preach the televised services.

As planned, on our anniversary Sunday, I was the worship leader for all the services, and Elmer preached. I announced the fact that Debra Sue and I would leave that evening on a Quantas flight from San Francisco to Auckland, New Zealand. That was not big news because we had announced it in our electronic newsletter. I also said that I was moving into semi-retirement, and that Elmer would be the full-time teaching pastor for the church.

94

10.

New Beginnings

While in New Zealand, Debra Sue and I talked constantly about my becoming semi-retired while she would continue to work full time. I had started keeping a journal when Elyse and I were students at Pepperdine. I looked back over my journal entries in the evenings in New Zealand after touring during the day while Debra Sue posted that day's pictures and videos on our web page. She pressed me to turn my journal into an autobiography. She said it should read like a literary selfie. I told her about how I was looking forward to slowing down.

Before we left for New Zealand, I asked Fred to arrange for my belongings in my church office to be boxed up and put in my home office. I told him that Elmer could move into my office as soon as he was ready. When Debra Sue and I got home, I knew what was waiting for me in my office. I did not touch the boxes for almost a week. I focused upon catching up on correspondence and returning phone calls. From Kansas City, I got a message from the current pastor of my old church that Lettie had died in her sleep at the retirement home where she had lived for more than twenty years. She was 107. I asked her pastor, Hank Robinson, if she had shared an Internet secret regarding Lettie's dead cousin. When he said no, I didn't think Lettie would mind if I shared the secret with him. He laughed and asked if Debra Sue and I would mind if he anonymously "lurked" with us. I told him to feel free, and that he could probably pass on the secret to his successor.

Something else happened while we were in New Zealand. Nancy Wells had died almost a month before we returned. Fred had seen to it that no one had notified us because he wanted us to enjoy our time down under. The day after we returned, Debra Sue and I went to John and Nancy's home, and we spent the better part of the day with John. He was obviously feeling lost, as though someone had amputated and discarded a part of him. We mixed our descriptions of New Zealand with memories of Nancy and John. He said he planned to sell the house and either get a small apartment or move into a retirement community.

I still had my key to the church, so two or three times a week I would go there to pray. Sometimes Elmer would join me, and from time to time we would have extended conversations after we prayed together. Ethylene joined the staff part-time, coordinating community outreach programs. Debra Sue continued to work full-time as Minister of Christian Education.

Almost daily, Debra Sue urged me to work on converting my journal into an autobiography. Reluctantly, I agreed. I began to enjoy fleshing out old journal entries with more details from other records and our memories. In my files, I found an outline I had started decades earlier for a book on Biblical Theology. I began to go back and forth between the two books, working on one or the other, depending on my mood.

Elmer had been leading the church for over a year when he joined me very early one morning for prayer. After about an hour, he invited me to join me in the office. Fred was not there yet.

After we sat down, Elmer led off the conversation. "Has Fred told you that he was retiring soon?"

I nodded. "He and Charlene had lunch with Debra Sue and I last Saturday. They want to do some traveling, I think."

"How long have Fred and Charlene been married?"

I looked up at the ceiling to arrange my memories. "Fred's first wife died a few years before I met him. He sort of re-connected with Charlene at their thirtieth high school reunion. They didn't date in high school, but they had classes together. Fred told me that there were sparks when they sat together at their reunion. They drove to Reno and eloped a month later, and I didn't even know he was married until he introduced her after church a week later."

Elmer smiled. "That sounds like Fred." He paused. "I'm glad you were here praying this morning because there's something I've been wanting to ask you about."

"What's that?"

"When I was meeting with you and the Elders before I was hired, you said that it seemed as though this facility was being properly utilized to capacity, and as this congregation continues to grow, that the leadership will have to consider either moving to a larger facility or launch satellite congregations."

I nodded. "That's right."

"Did you seriously consider either of those options?"

"Of course. Debra Sue and I discuss everything related to the church, and we have prayed about it extensively."

"Have you come to any conclusions?"

I shook my head. "Conclusions, no, but we see pathways."

"Pathways?"

"This congregation sits on this land because of the generosity of John and Nancy Wells, along with some others. If God wants this congregation to relocate, He will soon provide the finances and/or the land for that to happen."

"Do you think it will happen soon?"

I shook my head. "No. In all of our prayers, we've not seen a clear path in that direction. This amount of land in this location would today cost five times as much as it did originally. With God, all things are possible, but there does not seem to be a clear path in that direction. It seems far more likely that, before the end of this year, we will have our first satellite congregation."

"So, you think we'll have a satellite congregation later this year?"

I nodded. "It seems likely." I paused. "Are you familiar with the term, 'chumming?'"

Elmer nodded. "I've been known to go after some trout in the Sierras. Chumming is not allowed, however."

I was amused. "I don't know if you'd get jail time if you did, but we're talking about fishing for people in this case."

"What did you have in mind?"

I paused again. "Are you aware of how many people in this area are de-churched?"

Elmer shook his head. "No, are there quite a few? I understand the term to refer to those who used to go to church but have stopped for a variety of reasons."

"A long time ago I served on the School Board, and I still have quite a few friends in the school district. It seems as though there are quite a number of people who say, 'I used to go to such-and-such church, but I stopped going because...' and then give a reason. I've prayed about the idea of our renting an empty storefront, and later doing some skilled advertising aimed at people who are among the so-called 'de-churched.'"

"Where would we get staffing?"

"James Fields has his M.Div. from Fullbrite, and I think he and LaVonne would welcome the chance to launch another congregation, particularly if the worship is video-fed so that they can focus on ministries beyond worship. It would not be chumming, exactly, but it would mean starting a congregation with people who have broken away from church life."

Elmer was smiling. "I think this is a great idea, Frank. I'll ask James and LaVonne if they are interested." He stood up. "Have you had breakfast?"

I looked at my watch. "Knowing Debra Sue, she probably has breakfast almost ready." I took out my phone. "I'll see you Sunday, Elmer."

"See you Sunday."

As I left his office, I dialed. "Good morning, my love."

"Good morning."

"I'm leaving the church in a few minutes. Can I take you out to breakfast, or have you already started?"

"Let's eat out. You need a new pair of shoes, and there's sweaters on sale in several stores. I want to get a couple of new ones for the coming winter."

"Good idea! We'll go shopping after breakfast. I'll see you in a few minutes."

"Okay."

Twenty minutes later, we were in The Brown Sugar Kitchen. After we placed our orders, Debra Sue reached across the table to take my hand. "Frank, after the anniversary weekend, I want to retire and spend more time with you."

My smile felt big. "Wonderful! With the retirement funds that John and Nancy helped us set up long ago, we'll have plenty of income."

She nodded. "Did you see Elmer this morning?"

"Yes. After praying together for a while, we went to the office and talked. We're going to launch a satellite congregation. I think maybe we'll ask James and LaVonne to lead it."

She nodded. "I think he'll like that – in fact, I think they'll both love it."

Our breakfasts came, and we ate silently for a while. "Frank, when I looked into the study yesterday, it seemed like you were working pretty energetically. What were you so focused on?"

I chewed and swallowed. "Since last month, I've stopped making entries in my journal, and since then I've been adding entries to my autobiography. That doesn't take long, so it seems like the Holy Spirit has got me fired up to complete my book on Theology. That's probably what you saw me working on."

"That's great! Now, let's get your shoes first. There's a place down on Market that recently opened up. I'm going to treat you to a custom-fitted pair of shoes, Frank."

"Custom fitted?"

She nodded. "They laser-scan each foot, and then they 3-D print your shoes. David Eng says they feel marvelous on your feet."

I was amused. "This ought to be an interesting experience!"

When we got home that afternoon, my phone rang. It was James Fields. "Good afternoon, James! Pastor Elmer and I were talking about you this morning!"

"I know! He told me that you suggested that LaVonne and I start a satellite congregation. Do you really think we can do this, Pastor Frank?"

I sat down in my living room, in my recliner. "Absolutely! Of all the people I know, I think you and LaVonne are the most able to do this. Some of the largest congregations in the country have video-connected satellites. As I'm sure Pastor Elmer told you, we're going to focus on the de-churched. You and LaVonne can lead local worship that is wrapped around Elmer's messages. Just like other churches with satellites, sometimes your congregation will join the singing of the home congregation, but not always. You and LaVonne can focus upon prayers and fellowship, including Bible studies. You'll have the freedom to shape what you do with your own congregation, but you two will attend staff meetings on the hill once a week. I hope you two will pray about it before making a decision."

"We'll do that, Pastor Frank, and thank you! By the way, Pastor Elmer told us that we might not be the only satellite congregation that's launched this year."

"Really?"

"Yes! He said that after he talked with you this morning, he got a call from Lighthouse Chinese Community Church. They want to offer two of our services via video link to their schedule."

I was stunned. "All that God does, God does well."

+ + +

Preparations for the 30th anniversary worship service began early in the previous summer. We considered in the Spring about having the celebration service in the park or outside on our own property. In the end, we decided to hold a single service inside, with the video monitors and speakers activated not only in the sanctuary, but in all the classrooms, the meeting rooms, and the fully expanded dining room. Even the monitors in the kitchen were turned on in case anyone wanted to be in there. Elmer was the key to all the planning.

The two relatively new satellite congregations also prepared for larger crowds than usual. We planned to have the satellites offer celebrations of the Lord's Supper, while on our main campus, we would be baptizing thirty-seven people. The timing might have been tricky, but the details were worked out.

At the new high school's location, two blocks away, the land was cleared, but construction had not begun. We got permission to have overflow parking there, and we arranged for shuttles to go back and forth. I was excited with all the plans being made, even though I was not involved much in the preparations.

Debra Sue had more energy and stamina than I did, of course. In mid-August, Debra Sue came into my office in the evening. "Let's eat out tonight, Frank. Except for a brief lunch, I've been at the church since eight this morning. I've started a fire in our fireplace. Let's relax for a while with some cold drinks, and then we'll head down to Jack London Square. I've made reservations at the Seafood Grill."

I followed her into the living room, and we sat down on the sofa. She already had a pitcher of iced tea and glasses sitting on the coffee table. After we silently enjoyed our tea and watched the fire for a few minutes, she spoke softly. "This afternoon, I helped rearrange and clean up the cry room. We could have a crowd there too on our Anniversary Sunday." She paused. "Pastor Elmer has sent a blanket email to all the families with pre-teen and younger children. He's asking them to consider worshiping out on the lawn under the old tent. Surprisingly, it is still very usable. Middle School and High School youth are being asked to worship near the front in the sanctuary to encourage their friends who are getting baptized."

I pondered all of this silently. "When we got here thirty years ago, we didn't have so much as a glimmer of all of this taking place. Our Master knew, of course." She snuggled up against me. "When I was praying this morning after you left, I think the Lord gave me an intriguing suggestion."

She turned to looking at me. "What?"

"Why don't we reserve a sleeper cabin on a train going east and spend Christmas in Kansas City? We've still got a couple of dozen friends at that church, and Pastor Glenn Root has invited us to visit twice in the last three years."

I could tell Debra Sue liked the idea. "That sounds wonderful! Instead of your children coming here, we'll go out there. I'm sure I can get us a nice suite to stay in." She put her hand on my knee. "I would love to go to Nashville for New Years' Eve! We could use a good dose of country music!"

I remember that I chuckled at that idea. "If we go that far south, I'm sure we can make train connections to return out west to Los Angeles, and then we can take the coastal train back up here to the Bay Area." I swallowed some tea. "It's August, so we have plenty of time to plan our trip."

She spoke more quietly. "Frank, I probably don't have to ask, but have you ever mentioned to anyone our incident thirty years ago, when I was shot?"

The memory flooded back into my mind. "No. Why are you asking now, after all these years?"

"This morning I went into the sanctuary to pray, and suddenly that memory began to fill my mind. I talked to the Lord about it, of course, but throughout the day today that memory has been tugging on the edge of my thoughts. Could God be getting us ready for something, do you think?"

I drank a final swallow of my glass of tea and put it down. "It's possible, of course. Let's refresh our memories over dinner. I'm getting hungry."

She put her glass down. "Me too, but let's go to the bedroom first. I've got that blood-stained blouse on the top shelf of our closet. Let's look at it."

We got up, and we went to our bedroom. Debra Sue went to our closet and got out the small flat box that she had kept up there for nearly thirty years. To the best of my knowledge, I don't think she had ever opened it after we moved into our Oakland home.

On our bed, she opened the slightly dusty box. I touched the clear plastic bag inside the box, letting my fingers lightly caress the plastic above the blood-stained hole. My memories became as clear as those of earlier that day.

Debra Sue reached for my fingers, touching them lightly. "Was it like yesterday? Do you remember what you said and did?"

I nodded. "Yes, it's like it happened moments ago." I paused. "Coming into the house, there was a strange smell, and you asked me about it. We saw someone in a hood come toward us with a gun, and as I looked at the gun, it fired. I saw the flash and turned towards you, and you were falling. I saw blood coming from your chest, and as I followed you down I screamed 'No!'"

There in our Oakland bedroom, our hands touching, I looked into Debra Sue's eyes. "I looked up to see the shooter swinging the gun towards me. I heard myself say, 'In the name of Jesus may the Earth swallow you and leave no trace.' It seems as surreal remembering it all now as it seemed then. As the shooter dropped into the floor, I heard a man's voice scream, his arms went into the air, and he disappeared into the floor with the gun. I looked at you, and your eyes were closed. I was dumbfounded. I put my hands between your breasts over this hole and the blood. 'Jesus!' I think I practically shouted. 'In your name, please deliver us from this evil,' I said, and I closed my eyes. I don't know how long I knelt there. Then you began to stir."

Debra Sue took my fingers and kissed them. "When I opened my eyes, I was looking up at your face. All I could say was, 'Praise Jesus! I'm alive! I sat up. Then I told you again, 'I'm alive!' and told you that I had seen you, watching that man drop through the floor into the Earth, and then we were looking at each other." She paused. "When I took this off, it was bloody and had a hole in it, but I had no wound. The bullet must has entered me just below my bra, but there wasn't even any blood on it, I don't think."

I shook my head. "I don't remember there being any blood on it either. God has done some amazing things over the three decades since, but I wonder why this memory is coming back to us so vividly again now? Let's put this away and go eat."

She nodded. "Right." As we stood up, we put our arms around one another and held each other for a while.

The remaining two weeks of August went by very quickly. Debra Sue and I had lunch twice with Pastor Elmer and Ethelene Hanson. James and LaVonne Fields took Debra Sue and me to dinner, reporting that their first worship service at Oakland Community Bible Church was attended by 67 people. We encouraged James and LaVonne and gave them a few suggestions for the Anniversary service coming up.

Finally, Labor Day weekend arrived. We drove to the church an hour early, and at the invitation from a member of the church who lived across the street, we parked in their driveway. There were already a half dozen cars at one end of the parking lot. Debra Sue and I joined Elmer and Ethelene in the front row of the sanctuary to pray.

The worship service began with an upbeat praise song, led by a slightly larger than usual praise team. As the song concluded, Debra Sue and I together went to the podium to welcome everyone and offer an opening prayer. There did not appear to be any empty seats. "Welcome everyone. For those of you who do not know us, we are Debra Sue and Frank Frazee. Thirty years ago, we...."

About ten yards in front of us, a man stepped into the center aisle. He dropped the coat off his shoulders, revealing what appeared to be explosives. He yelled, "Allahu Akbar!"

Debra Sue, much to my surprise, loudly said with me, "In the name of Jesus may the Earth swallow you and leave no trace!" Without another word, a surprised terrorist vanished through the floor. Debra Sue and I looked at one another, and, together again we said, "Praise God! Praise God!"

Members of the praise team picked up on what we said, and about a dozen or so times all of us were calling out, "Praise God! Praise God!" Several in the congregation picked up on it, and for another minute or so, the chant continued.

Finally, I held up my hand. The praises subsided. "We're indeed here to praise God, not to mourn the loss of a terrorist. It's appropriate we're all praising God!" I paused. "As I started to say a few minutes ago, Debra Sue and I, along with Nancy and John Wells, launched this congregation under a tent on top of this hill thirty years ago today." There was applause. "I have retired from being the pastor, and Debra Sue and I are enjoying some retirement time together. I trust that God will not allow further interruptions. My beloved wife will now offer our opening prayer."

She smiled. "Let's offer our praises and thanks to God in prayer." As I expected, she prayed a beautiful and appropriate prayer, and then we sat down. The worship service proceeded as though we had been merely interrupted by a scheduled drama with special effects. As the second praise song began, an usher came down the aisle and retrieved the coat that the terrorist had worn. The "usher" was Gary Thomason, now a lieutenant in the Oakland Police Department. He knew that what we had witnessed was not a drama with special effects. Near the rear, he beaconed to a woman to join him in the foyer. He told the Police Chief that what she had seen was not a staged drama. They discussed it in hushed tones there in the foyer for about five minutes before he returned to where he had been sitting, while she took out her phone.

There were no further interruptions, and the worship service proceeded as we had planned. After the service, Gary spoke to me quietly. "You've known the Police Chief, Linda Purviance, since she joined the congregation several years ago. She has gone down to City Hall. She wants to call on you and Debra Sue in your home this afternoon at 2:00, to talk to you about what happened this morning."

I nodded. "Would you like to join us, Gary?"

He responded solemnly. "Yes, I would, Pastor Frank, if you don't mind."

I shook my head. "We won't mind at all."

+ + +

That evening, Debra Sue and I watched at home as the Police Chief held a press conference. She was entirely professional. "Before I answer a few questions, I have a statement to make." Everyone became quiet. "This morning at a few minutes past eleven, more than a thousand people witnessed something extraordinary, something that many would say is impossible. Countless thousands more witnessed this on video, distributed live from Hilltop Christian Center. I call your attention to the video display beside me." Almost a minute of the worship service was played back. "First of all, this was not a staged drama. Facial recognition software identifies the man seen in the video as Omar Khayyam, and yes, it is the same name as a famous mathematician in history. This particular man was previously connected to some extremist activities."

She waited until murmuring subsided. "As I said, this was not a staged drama. I have been a member of the congregation for several years. This afternoon, our crime scene scientists have examined both the coat that the man was wearing and the floor where he disappeared. The flooring of that church is laid on a slab of steel re-enforced concrete attached to pilings going deep into the hill. We have examined the blueprints for the building, and I have personally talked to the contractor who built the facility. There is not a trap door, and there is no possibility of a trap door where the man disappeared. Naturally, there will be those who argue for some kind of conspiracy regarding this incident, but law enforcement cannot help that."

She picked up a bottle of water and drank. "There was evidence contained within the coat that was left behind, and if it leads to any further things to report, I will provide an update. All official information regarding this event is being passed through my office. If someone reports anything I have not released to the media, they are lying. Now I will answer a few questions."

"Has the flooring been examined by the city's laboratory?"

"Yes. Several boards from the aisle of the church have been removed for analysis. The church also supplied us with a board from the church's storage that was saved for possible future use. We sent one of the evidence boards to the FBI laboratory in San Francisco, along with half of the unused board supplied to us for comparison. As of ten minutes before this press conference, both labs have confirmed that there is no evidence in the wood of the man, his clothing, or what appeared to be the explosives."

"Have either of the two speakers indicated why they spoke to the terrorist as they did?"

"Frank and Debra Sue Frazee were the speakers at the podium at the time of this incident. Thirty years ago, they helped launch Hilltop Christian Center. I talked with them at length early this afternoon. They indicated that what they said was purely a natural reflex. They think they said the same thing together because they have known one another for more than thirty years. One more question. Yes?" She pointed.

"Do you personally think this was a miracle?"

There was hushed silence as she hesitated. "Many times, I have heard Pastor Frank say, 'All that God does, God does well.' I once heard him preach a sermon on the passage in Matthew's gospel where Jesus curses a fig tree. This morning, Pastor Frank and Debra Sue said a simple prayer. It appeared to those of faith that God responded.... That's all, unless further evidence becomes available."

After watching that press conference together and ever since, Debra Sue and I have stood mute.

11.
Miracle Church

Debra Sue and I were looking forward to a quiet retirement, but that would have to wait until we could move beyond the miracle. I wanted to focus on my writing, but evidently God had other plans. Countless times I had told Debra Sue we had to trust God with everything. The process we faced seemed daunting.

Monday morning, Debra Sue and I had an early breakfast and went to the church to pray. Most of our prayers were silent. Shortly after sunrise, we heard the doors behind us opening, and we knew who was here. Both Elmer and Earlene joined us in the front row of the sanctuary. After a while, they moved to sit on the kneeling cushions so that they could face us. I looked at them soberly. "Good morning. We've been expecting you two to join us. I imagine the two of you have questions, don't you?"

Elmer nodded. "In my much shorter professional career, I've witnessed a couple of miraculous healings, but absolutely nothing like what I saw on the monitor yesterday."

Debra Sue handed Ethelene a small flat box. "You two can look at this right now, but when we leave, we need to have you forget that you ever saw it."

Elmer watched as Ethelene opened the box and took out the vacuum-sealed plastic bag. She looked up at Debra Sue. "Are those blood stains around that hole?"

"Yes."

"Is it a bullet hole?"

Debra Sue nodded. "Yes."

Ethelene's mouth dropped open. "You wore this, and you were shot?"

Debra Sue nodded and told Elmer and Ethelene the story as briefly as she could.

Elmer was as stunned as his wife. "The two of you used that same prayer yesterday."

I nodded. "Yes. We heard ourselves saying it, in a detached kind of way, almost like a reflex."

Elmer was silent as he considered what we had told them. "I feel as though I have to carry the ball for this. Is that agreeable to both of you?"

I nodded and pointed to the box, now in Elmer's lap. "When that happened, we resolved not to speak about it with anyone. We talked about sharing the story with John and Nancy Wells, but you're the first to hear it. We've kept silent about what happened in our Kansas City home, but this was witnessed by thousands, although those who saw it on video can claim editing or even a conspiracy."

Elmer was solemn. "That's why I think I should carry the ball. I need to discuss it as a sermon next Sunday. I've decided to keep the sermon's focus upon what God did and not mention either of you. I'll mention a miraculous healing I witnessed, and without mentioning you two by name, I will mention the earthquake that occurred while the pilings for this building were being cast. David Eng told me that story, and I'll pass it on as his. I'll call him this morning and tell him I'm going to share the story without mentioning you two by name."

Debra Sue smiled. "David Eng is one of the best communicators I've ever met. He's as open as the occasion calls for, but he knows how to avoid answering a question if necessary while still being polite. There was a news segment on him one evening, and the journalist asked him some very provocative questions. Unfazed, David provided a detailed answer with many unrequested details while not actually answering the journalist's questions. Throughout the interview, David was polite and congenial, but he hardly answered any of the questions that he was asked."

Elmer nodded. "I like David. He's very intuitive. I won't have to mention discretion because he'll know I'm going to be discrete." The pastor paused. "I'm going to use John 14 as my sermon's scripture foundation. Do other passages come to mind for you, Frank?"

I closed my eyes a moment. "That's probably the best scripture I could use if I were preaching on getting expected answers to prayer. There's another passage that I've only rarely heard preached in my experience, and it can be applied more directly to this incident. Most lay people are unfamiliar with it, and it is thought-provoking because it seems to show another side of Jesus. Since you want to keep the focus upon God, it will definitely suit your purpose."

Ethelene had a perplexed look on her face. "What passage is that, Frank?"

"After Palm Sunday, but before Maundy Thursday, Jesus cursed a fig tree. According to Matthew's account, in chapter 21, the result of the curse was seen immediately."

"Oh my! I didn't think of that!"

Elmer nodded. "God's response to yesterday's prayer was certainly immediate! As I think about it, I know I've never used that incident in a sermon until now, and I don't think I've ever read or heard a sermon on that passage." He handed the box to me, and I handed it back to Debra Sue.

I stood up as Debra Sue closed up the box and retied the ribbon around it. I looked at my watch. "I would imagine this building is going to be inundated with the media as soon as you unlock the outer door near the offices. As you probably noticed, we parked down towards the eastern end of the building. Debra Sue and I can go into the prayer room upstairs for a while. We can see the parking lot from up there, and when it looks like the coast is clear, we'll take our car and go get brunch."

Elmer nodded. "That sounds like a plan. I would imagine the media will want to see that patch of bare concrete where the aisle's flooring has been removed. You two can head toward the elevator, and Ethelene and I will take our time going into the office. Fred isn't retiring until the first of November, so he'll be unlocking things in less than ten minutes. Maybe he already has."

Debra Sue and I headed to the east hallway and the elevator. When we got upstairs and went into the prayer room, we looked out the window. There were several news vans, along with more than a dozen cars parked in the lot. There were also a few dozen people standing around and talking. Debra Sue pointed. "There comes Fred. That's his white Subaru."

Two men got out. "Fred must have picked up Grandy this morning." As the two men walked towards the front doors, Grandy took out his phone. I chuckled. "I know who Grandy is calling."

"Who?"

"One of Grandy's grandsons is a police sergeant. Watch! There'll be police cars here for crowd control in a minute or two."

Debra Sue looked at her watch, and we waited. When police cars approached from both directions, she looked at her watch again. "Four minutes! Three patrol cars! Look! Two cars are staying close to the driveways. I wonder who is.... That's Gary and his new partner, Alex."

I started toward the door. "If we're quiet and a little sneaky, we can watch what's happening in the sanctuary without being seen." I heard Debra Sue giggle. I stage whispered. "I know! Who'd of thought we might get caught sneaking around in the church we built?"

Silently, we snuck into the east transept balcony. Seated, we could lean over and watch below the railing through the grill. There were videos and stills being made of the concrete base of the floor, where part of the flooring had been removed. They talked too quietly for us to hear them. Two of them stamped on the floor in several places. Evidently, they were hoping to hear evidence of emptiness under the floor. Suddenly, some of the church's lighting came on. I whispered. "Grandy must have turned them on."

She nodded and pointed, as Gary and Alex quietly came in from the rear, circled around to the front, and waited. Debra Sue whispered softly. "I think Gary and Alex are making sure no one tries to hide and stay behind."

We heard the door open behind us, and we turned to see Grandy coming in. He didn't look down at us but came and stood nearby. He spoke softly. "Only the main front doors are unlocked, and Fred is keeping track of how many are inside. Gary and Alex will see to it that they all leave. My grandson is watching the security monitors."

I nodded. "Good job, Grandy, I knew you'd stay on top of things."

"One guy asked me where the basement stairs were. I told him that if he finds a basement to let me know, because in all my years here I've never cleaned one."

I smiled. "So, you've never found either our secret basement or our dungeon?"

He stifled a laugh. "No, Pastor Frank! I've not found a state-of-the-art observatory either!" He paused. "Gary and Alex are shaking their heads at some of them and pointing towards the rear exits. I guess they're all leaving. I'm going back downstairs." Grandy turned and left.

Silently, Debra Sue and I stayed up there until Grandy turned the main lights off again. I gestured towards the door. "Let's go back to the prayer room and watch until everything seems clear," I whispered.

Gary and Alex's car did not leave until the last of the media vehicles had left. As we took the elevator down, and we decided to go home. As the garage door was closing behind us, someone ducked under the door and approached us. "Mr. & Mrs. Frazee, I'm Bob Stout. I'm a free-lance journalist. I need to ask you a few questions."

"We have agreed with the senior pastor of Hilltop Christian Center, whose name is Elmer Hanson, to let him deal with the media. My wife and I have nothing to say to you either on or off the record."

"But…"

"No." I took out my phone. "Alex, this is Pastor Frank Frazee. I hope you and Gary are still in the area. As our garage door was closing behind us, a man identifying himself as a free-lance journalist named Bob Stout ducked under our garage door and said he wanted to ask us a few questions. I've said no, but he is insistent."

"We're in the neighborhood. Don't go inside. When we honk our horn twice, open the garage door."

"Okay, thanks." I put my phone away and looked at the man. I stared him down, and he stared back. A moment or two later, we heard a car honk twice, I put my thumb against a scanner by the door, and I said, "outer door open."

As the garage door opened again, Gary and Alex were standing there. The man protested. "I'm a licensed journalist, and

I have a second amendment right to seek out and report the news."

As Alex approached the man with handcuffs, Gary nodded. "You have your second amendment right so long as you otherwise stay within your limits as prescribed by law. When you snuck into their garage and demanded information from them, that can be construed as senior abuse, so you are under arrest. The rest will be between your lawyer and the district attorney."

Alex put plastic cuffs on the intruder and looked at me. "I saw the worship service at your satellite church with Pastor James Fields. I'm sure we'll worship there again. It's nice to meet you, sir."

"It's nice to meet you too, Alex. I've known your partner a long time."

"Yes, sir, so he has told me." Alex took the man to their patrol car and put him in the back seat. They waved as they got in. I closed the garage door, and we went inside.

Over lunch, we discussed what had just happened. I guess I was pretty emphatic. "From this day forwards, let's be sure when the doorbell rings who it is. If it is the media, we'll tell them that any information they need can be gained at the church."

She bit into her sandwich and chewed, nodding her head. After swallowing, she spoke in a voice that told me that she was really upset. "You don't have to tell me that twice, Frank. That was probably just the beginning."

It was. That week after the miracle, there were journalists at our door at least once a day. Even by the middle of September, they were still showing up regularly. When they would show up at the church on Sundays, we had a secret signal for the ushers, and media people were simply told that if they were not there to worship God, they could leave. As Pastor Elmer put it in the announcements more than once, "We have a second amendment right to worship as a spiritual community without interference by others." Almost daily there were news segments regarding the "miracle church," covering what had happened from various perspectives.

During the third week of October, we spent five days at a bed and breakfast at Crater Lake National Park in Southern Oregon. It was a first for both of us, and Debra Sue enjoyed pursuing her photography skills with me. I simply enjoyed God's handiwork. The beauty of that park is seldom reported in travel brochures. It was good to get away.

When we got back home, there was a letter from the courthouse, including a letter from the Oakland District Attorney's office and, in the same envelope, a letter from Bob Stout. He humbly apologized for being overly zealous in his desire to get our story. He asked us not to press charges against him. I called District Attorney Dudley Hughes and told him we would not press charges.

I have continued to make entries into my personal journal, which has become my autobiography. Debra Sue wants me to keep it up to date.

I continued to preach three or four services every month. When Elmer wanted to take a week off to celebrate his 25th anniversary with Ethelene, I preached all the services on that Sunday. I was totally exhausted the next day, but I felt great otherwise.

We held a big party for Fred as he retired. His retirement gift from the church was a Holy Land cruise scheduled for the following Spring. He and his wife were thrilled. At the party, Fred introduced his own replacement. He had suggested John Simons to the Elders, and after a few interviews, John had been hired.

One of his interviews was with Elmer and me. Elmer made it a congenial meeting over lunch. "John, why don't you describe briefly how you got to be where you are now, both physically and spiritually."

John glanced at me and focused upon Elmer. "After getting my bachelor's degree in English and Computer Science, I went to work for the online edition of the Bee in San Francisco. They stopped printing the newspaper several years ago, as you know. That was an easy decision because in high school, I had developed a gift for speed reading. I can read the entire Sunday online edition of the Bee in less than a half-hour with 90% comprehension. When I slowed down to my analytical speed, I edited for grammar, spelling, style, and other factors as a copy editor, and I could do it for a 2,500-word article in ten minutes. When I told them I had decided to join the Navy, they offered to double my salary if I stayed, but I had already made my decision."

I was curious. "Why did you join the Navy if you had a well-paid job doing something you could do well?"

"In reality, Pastor Frank, I was looking for a challenge."

"Were you a Christian at that point?"

He shook his head. "No. Neither of my parents were religious, and at the Bee, I found there was open hostility to religion, at least in the area where I worked. Anyway, in the Navy I went for Seal Training, and I passed. For fifteen years, I moved up in the ranks, doing missions I probably will never be able to talk about. Last Spring, I was seriously injured, and now there are some major bones in my body that have metal replacements. I can no longer go out on missions. As I look back on nearly all of those missions, I can see God nudging me repeatedly. Late last December I was leading a mission when, in an incident when I thought we were all going to die, I felt a hand on my shoulder that was bigger than mine, but I couldn't see it. I heard a voice say, 'Relax, John, I've got this one.' The next thing I knew, my entire unit was out of danger."

"So, you completed your mission?" Elmer shifted in his seat.

John nodded. "Oh, yes. When I went on leave afterward, I went to see Fred Webster. He and I have known each other since I was a teenager, when he and his father got me out of a tough scrape. After I told him some of my struggles, he shared with me some of the things he has learned from you, Pastor Frank."

I was somewhat surprised, so I smiled. "That's interesting, because Fred almost never mentions anything in particular regarding my sermons."

John again nodded. "That's Fred. Anyway, back on this last Labor Day weekend, my wife and I went to church with Fred and his wife. My wife's name is Sarah. She was a Cobra pilot when I met her. That Sunday I was sitting in an aisle seat when that guy stepped into the aisle. When he dropped his coat, and I saw the explosives, all my training kicked in, and I tensed up. I was going to jump him, but Sarah put her hand on my knee just as the guy dropped through the floor. I felt that same big invisible hand on my shoulder, and suddenly I was enveloped in a sense of peace that totally saturated me."

Elmer nodded. "On the phone you told me that the first time you worshiped with us, you experienced what the Jews call 'shalom.' It means completeness, soundness, welfare, and peace. It is often used both as a greeting and as a farewell."

Again, John nodded. "Fred and I went with our wives upstairs into your prayer room. We were there more than two hours. Then, over lunch, Fred told me he was retiring from being the church's secretary and business manager. He asked me if I was interested. I've been praying about it ever since. I think this is where I belong from this point on." He paused. "Pastor Frank, Fred tells me you've been working on a couple of books. If you're willing, I'd like to be your editor."

I think my mouth dropped open for a moment. "That's very generous of you, John, but I could not pay you very much."

He smiled. "That's okay. You and Pastor Elmer have already paid me with some of your sermons. My wife is seeing positive changes in me that I don't see in myself, at least not yet. We sat in the back when you did a small wedding here last June. She and I are trying to build each other up in holiness now, and our bonds are stronger than ever."

By the time Elmer and I had spent another hour or so with John, we were both positive that John was the logical replacement for Fred, and we were both certain as well that God was at work in the whole process.

+ + +

I have found in retirement that I have broadened my ministry of encouragement, and Debra Sue has done the same. Each time I have an opportunity to offer spiritual support or encouragement to someone new, I put them on my calendar to see them again within ten days to two weeks. Without planning to, I eased into this by checking in with Elmer regularly, giving him encouragement.

One Friday, I drove down to Oakland Community Bible Church. That storefront church continues to thrive. I recognized the car by the front door, so I went in, and I walked directly to the church's office. James Fields looked up. "Good morning, Pastor Frank! This is a nice surprise!" We shook hands.

"When I was praying for you and LaVonne this morning, I got the impression that I should drop by for a visit, James."

"Thank you, we welcome all the prayers we can get!" He gestured towards a chair near his desk, and we both sat down.

"James, what's the latest? How's the church doing?"

"We have new visitors almost every Sunday, and most of them come back at least once. I think in January we'll hold a special baptismal service up at the main campus. In these first few months, I developed a group of more than twenty people that are ready to follow the Lord's example."

I nodded. "Excellent! I'm sure pastor Elmer can help you and encourage you with that. There's a church in Indianapolis that assigns a mentor to each new member, whether they join with or without baptism. Pastor Elmer is going to start doing it. The mentors are established active members, and they help the new members get involved in church life for the first year after they join. After that, it is up to each mentor to decide whether they want to continue the connection."

"This sounds like a great idea!" James took a pencil and jotted down some notes on a scratch pad. "I'll put this into my computer later when I share it with LaVonne. One of our main struggles right now is getting the administrative work done. I understand Fred has retired again."

"Yes, and his replacement is a Navy Seal named John."

"I talked with him on the phone last week."

"When my first wife and I started in Kansas City, our congregation was about the same size as yours. We got volunteers to come in a couple of days a week to get the chores done until we were big enough to hire some help. Just mention it on Sunday morning. You'll find that there are probably some people that are looking for opportunities to serve."

James scribbled more on his scratch pad. "I guess there are some who need the opportunity to serve just as I need the help."

"That's right. You and LaVonne showed your interest in serving the first Sunday you were with us on the hill under the tent. Experience has taught me that most people wait to be asked. You and LaVonne can discuss the potential you see in each of the people in your community. If you decide how someone can serve, don't use email or text. Don't call them on your computer or smart phone. Talk to them in person. It takes more effort, but you and LaVonne will get better results."

I spent another half-hour with James that day, and before I left, I prayed with him and for him. I followed a similar pattern when I visited Lighthouse Chinese Community Church. The pastor there was only a year younger than I am, and he had decided that all of their services would be via the video link with Pastor Elmer and Hilltop. I particularly enjoyed sharing faith with him and praying with him. Though we were practically the same age, we were from different cultural backgrounds. He fascinated me. After our first meeting, I resolved to learn how to pronounce his Chinese name properly. It is Zhang Jie. Most people did not try. It means "hero," but most simply called him Pastor Al. "Al" is a nickname he acquired as a teenager, because friends thought he looked like the actor, Al Molinaro.

Epilogue
by Debra Sue

A number of people attempted to promote their conspiracy theories regarding what happened at the thirtieth anniversary worship service. The media continued to press us for interviews for nearly a year. Before God called Frank home, we lived our lives even more fully than when we were working together.

I truly wish that Frank had continued to write after we agreed to stand mute regarding the very public miracle. I pushed him to continue writing, and he did for a while. Then I began keeping my own journal. There certainly has been a lot to write about. Frank was a clear and concise writer. Frank and I both grew fond of John Simons and his wife, Sarah. Whenever they came for dinner, she brought pies – marvelous pies.

With John's help, Frank finished his book on Biblical Theology. Pepperdine University published it about two years later. After a glowing and detailed review in *Christianity Today* magazine, many seminaries began adding Frank's book to their required reading lists.

One evening, after Frank revealed to John and Sarah that he had stopped making entries in his journal, John took me aside. "Debra Sue, I think it's important that you start your own journal. Don't worry about grammar, spelling, and style. When we publish Frank's autobiography after he goes home, you will have written – with my help – an epilogue regarding his final years."

I nodded and said, "Okay." As a woman, I see, analyze, and approach things differently. I hope this epilogue is not too long.

After Frank had made three encouragement visits to James and told me about them, I began inviting James and LaVonne over to our house for meals so that I could take a more active role in our "encouragement business." I suggested to Ethelene that there be monthly leadership conferences involving the staffs of Hilltop and its satellite congregations.

For six Labor Day weekends after the televised miracle, it was almost a ritual that news outlets reminded their subscribers of Hilltop's history and the miracle. Frank and I got in the habit of being "out of pocket" (unavailable) on Labor Day weekends. John Simons became a sideshow of sorts, since he was a witness sitting about ten feet from the miracle. I think he enjoys telling his side of the story.

One evening, John and Sarah were having dinner with us, and Frank looked at his watch. "John, ever since your friend installed that firewall for us on our computer, our problems have mostly cleared up, but in less than ten minutes our phone is going to ring. The computer picks it up, but every evening a call comes in at exactly 7:00. It's hard to believe that it's a common robocall, since there's stiff regulation on such things. What do you think?"

"Frank, let's go to your study. Log on as you usually do. I want to watch as the firewall my friend installed deals with the call."

As we went into the study, I activated the large wall monitor, so that we could all watch. John worked our keyboard and put the program's page on the display. At 7:00, the phone rang briefly, and then the program kicked in.

John smiled as we saw a logo appear next to the calling number. "This outfit is careful never to tap into anything related to a major industry or government entity. They only go after private citizens. I think my friend at Vandenberg will want to see this. May I use your house phone?" I nodded, and he picked up the handset and punched numbers. He put it on the speaker.

"Vandenberg Air Force Base, Lieutenant Sams."

"Hey Ron, this is John Simons."

"Hey, John, how do you like working for your church?"

John glanced up at us. "I love it. I'm at a retired pastor's house. Tigre Systems just called this number I'm on."

"They're an ugly outfit. ... Let me see something here." There was silence for several seconds while Ron worked at his computer. "How come they didn't get into your pastor's computer?"

"Larry Laraway installed one of his firewalls."

"That's a good thing." Ron paused. "... You know, John. It would be terrible for Tigre Systems if they made the mistake of trying to hack the IRS computer network."

A big smile spread across John's face. "In an outfit like Tigre Systems, no one would be that foolish, would they?"

"Do you think maybe someone there wants to examine their supervisor's tax returns anonymously?"

John laughed. "It would be a shame if someone was so foolish as to attempt such a hack, Ron."

"I agree, but a challenge is a challenge, John. I will not do anything illegal, you know that, but someone at Tigre Systems, who is new to the job might make a mistake like that."

"So, you'll be devious, but completely legal?"

"Of course! I promise."

"Thanks Ron! I'll see you next month at Paul's party."

"Right!"

The call ended. John stood up. "Sarah, I think we're all ready for some of your pie. I don't think Frank and Debra Sue will be getting any more calls from Tigre Systems. If I know Ron, tomorrow night's call from Tigre Systems won't even reach your phone. Their records will show no answer, as usual. The trap will be set." Frank and I looked at each other, and both of us were smiling.

As we ate our pie, I pulled up some of our pictures and videos from New Zealand for John and Sarah to see. Sarah was obviously fascinated. "That must be a really long flight!"

Frank nodded. "It's about thirteen and a half hours. Even though we flew business class, which is pretty comfortable, it was still a long flight."

John looked at his wife. "You've got an interesting look on your face that I rarely see, Sarah. What's going on inside that pretty head of yours?"

She smiled sweetly. "My uncle Bill's company has a Gulfstream that goes back and forth to their branches down under every week. Pastor Frank and Debra Sue could go with us if they wanted to."

I think Frank could see the excitement on my face. "Debra Sue, what do you think?"

I didn't hesitate. "Sure!"

Fred Webster agreed to fill in for John for three weeks in January which, in the Southern Hemisphere, is in the summer. Bill Hendrix's company not only flew us down there, but Sarah's uncle also supplied a luxury SUV and driver for us. Sarah and I bonded like sisters, and Frank and John were like brothers on a field trip. Sometimes we would spend a night or two with some of Frank's Anglican friends, but most of the time we preferred the excellent bed and breakfast facilities that were available nearly everywhere. After spending two weeks in New Zealand, we crossed the Tasman Sea and toured the east coast of Australia. I would have liked to spend more time there.

When we got back, Frank was hungry to catch up with the people in the Bay Area that he supported and encouraged. Whenever we said we were going to ride the BART, John wanted to go along as a sort of watch dog. If he could not get away from the church, he would ask one of his Navy buddies to go with us. Frank and I would have felt safe enough without an escort, but John wanted to do it.

One mid-September day Frank and I were in Golden Gate Park. More than a dozen people recognized us. As we were riding the BART under the bay back to Oakland, I mentioned it to him. "Frank, I think you're beginning to be pretty well-known in the Bay Area."

He shook his head. "I don't think so. We happened to run into some of our acquaintances, but that doesn't mean I'm becoming famous."

I glanced at our escort and driver, and he was smiling and shaking his head. I don't think Frank ever comprehended how many people loved him and appreciated him. His Biblical Theology book had already nearly sold out its second printing.

Over the next seven years, four times a year James Fields would was interviewing Frank for Internet presentations about a variety of subjects, each lasting almost an hour. Those videos were getting millions of views. When Frank preached for Pastor

Elmer two or three times each month, his sermons were downloaded thousands of times. Frank was not the least bit interested in how many people were hearing from him.

Frank was focused on just two things. He wanted God to continue to use him as long as possible. He also wanted to be a good husband to me. Despite our twenty-six-year age difference, my passion for Frank never lagged in the least, even when he was well into his nineties, and I was past seventy. He was my loving and doting husband and best friend every day.

Maybe it was because I had turned seventy, but after Frank's ninety-sixth birthday, we both seemed to slow down. Frank had tried using a cane a few times, but when we were at Glacier Point in Yosemite one Spring, he bought a beautiful walking stick. He did not take it out of the closet until after he turned ninety-six. Then he took it everywhere.

One evening after dinner, Frank was looking at the Digital Bee. "Debra Sue, have we ever gone to the Paramount Theater in Oakland?"

I shook my head. "We've talked about taking in a classic movie there, but we've never gone. Why, what's showing now?"

"They're showing 'Forrest Gump' there between now and Sunday. James and LaVonne told me one day that the Paramount is a beautifully restored Art-Deco theater. I'd like to see both the movie and the theater."

I nodded. "It sounds like an interesting change of pace, dear. Joey Donovan said that we could call him anytime we need a driver. I'll call him and see if he's available." As Frank nodded, I took out my phone and pushed numbers. "Joey? This is Debra Sue Frazee. How are you this evening?"

"I'm blessed, Mrs. Frazee. Would you like me to drive you somewhere?"

"As a matter of fact, Pastor Frank just now said he'd like to see 'Forrest Gump' at Oakland's Paramount Theater."

"Hold on, I'll look over the theater schedule." He paused for nearly a minute. "If I pick you up right away, we'll make the next show from the beginning and get back around ten. Will that be too late?"

"No, Joey, that will be fine. We'll see you in a few minutes."

When he rang our doorbell, Joey was wearing his Army uniform with a green beret. He was handsome! He drove us quickly to the theater, and he was able to park his SUV only about two blocks away. We were walking up Broadway, taking our time, when suddenly there were several other soldiers around us, with their backs to us, facing in all directions. A teenager, dressed in black with a red bandana, approached us. He spoke with a slight Hispanic accent. "Relax guys! We see you're escorting Pastor Frank Frazee. Several years ago, I was with my parents at Hilltop for worship when Pastor Frank and his wife sent that terrorist to hell. They're heroes to all of us. There'll be no trouble in this neighborhood tonight. I promise you!"

Joey spoke quietly. "You and your boys control this neighborhood?"

"Yeah, I'm Tommy Sands."

I recognized him. "Tommy, am I going to see you in church again soon?"

"You bet, Mrs. Frazee. I'll be there by Christmas, if not before."

"I'll look for you Tommy."

He smiled. "Okay, Mrs. Frazee." He turned and walked away.

Frank squeezed my hand. "I thought I recognized him. Was he in our Youth for Jesus group?"

I squeezed his hand back. "Yep."

At the late Christmas Eve service, Tommy approached me. "Mrs. Frazee, my boys and I are glad you and Pastor Frank like the Paramount. You and Pastor Frank will never need an escort. Even my gang's enemies respect you. There'll be no trouble from any of us."

"How long are you going to stay with your gang?"

He shook his head. "I don't know, Mrs. Frazee. Joey and some of his friends have talked to us a few times. They're trying to get me and some of my boys into the Marines, or maybe into Special Forces. I don't know, Mrs. Frazee. Please pray for us."

He turned and walked away quickly, and I simply called after him. "Merry Christmas, Tommy!" He waved above his head without turning.

Frank and I fell in love with the Paramount Theater, and we started going there regularly, though we moved a bit more slowly each time. For a few months, we sometimes caught glimpses of Tommy, and we waved to him. The following Spring, Joey told us that Tommy was in San Diego for Special Forces training. After that, from time to time, Tommy would attend a service wearing his uniform while on leave. A year later, Pastor Elmer presided at Tommy's wedding to a woman who he had met while getting his Seal training. She was a pilot, like Sarah Simons, only she flew jets of some kind. Frank and I corresponded with them for a while.

When Frank reached his centennial birthday, his birthday party was attended by more than a thousand people. Several people came from our church in Kansas City. Many of the retirees that attended joked with him, hoping that they would be as healthy as he was when they reached a hundred.

Frank went up on a platform to thank everyone. "First of all, I want to thank all of you for coming. I've outlived many of my friends, and I have outlived all of my children except my oldest son, Mark, who is here beside me. I'm also glad to see five of my grandchildren here and eleven of my great-grandchildren also, all but one of whom I'm meeting for the first time today." There was scattered applause. "Since Debra Sue and I have not had any children, all of those are from my first marriage to a woman named Elyse. As some of you know, it was Elyse who set Debra Sue and me up for our marriage."

He paused, and Mark handed Frank a glass of water. Frank drank several swallows. "Since I come from a large family, there are several of my nieces and nephews here, though I have outlived my siblings. The majority of you are associated either directly or indirectly with Hilltop Christian Center. Pastor Elmer told me a little while ago that he will probably retire next year. He and I have already gone fishing together a time or two." He paused to look around the room. "I'll say one more thing. For both my beloved Debra Sue and I, Jesus has been in our hearts as our Savior, best friend, and constant companion for as long as we can remember. If you don't have a solid relationship with God through Jesus, I strongly urge you to pursue that relationship. May God grant each and every one of you the vision to perceive

God's plans and purposes for you. May you have the faith to believe in and trust God with everything. Finally, may each of you have the courage to trust God to help you find the fulfilment of your lives."

As a standing ovation erupted from everyone there, Mark and I helped Frank return to his seat near the stage. That night, we were both exhausted and happy.

After Frank and I celebrated his one hundred third birthday, two weeks later he went home to Jesus.

Elmer and Ethelene helped me ship many of our possessions to Frank's grandchildren. Mark, Frank's son, said he already had all he wanted. The new pastor, Bill Lake, created a password-protected directory on the church computer, where we transferred all of Frank's and my files from our home computer. I sold our house, and I donated the proceeds from the sale to a scholarship fund established by the church. I have a small but nice apartment about two miles from the church. I spend time with people from the church nearly every day.

I'm approaching eighty now, and I suspect I'll be joining Frank and Elyse soon enough. Other than Jesus, Frank was my life's greatest blessing. I had two boyfriends in high school, and I almost married a man when I was at Brite Divinity School. Not one of those men loved me as tenderly and passionately as Frank did.

Frank had many gifts, and several limitations. He loved music, but when singing he was definitely not a musician. He was a natural diplomat, and his entire being was infused with a Christ-centered sense of ideals and morals. He was not what I would call a dreamer, but when he fulfilled his goals, the results had a lasting impact on many people. He had an excellent memory except for people's names. Both Elyse and I helped him with that. Although he could be a bit absent-minded. Once he zeroed in on his goal, his focus was unwavering.

Frank saw his purpose in life as helping people have a solid relationship with Jesus. He rescued people from time to time, and he did some charity work even beyond his role as a pastor. He preferred, however, to help people help themselves, so that they didn't need him to rescue them.

When he wasn't speaking in public, Frank was usually soft-spoken. He had strong opinions, and I happily played second fiddle to his passion for the church. I still wish we could have had children. We talked more than once about adopting.

We had a great marriage and a great life. As Frank said countless times, "All that God does, God does well."

Other Books by James J. Stewart
Available at Amazon

Christian Inspiration, Study, and Poetry

**Faith and Yosemite:
Fourth Edition**
*[Christian poetry with
pictures of Yosemite]*

**Seed Thoughts for
Christian Prayer
and Meditation**
[Workbook]

Faith Fuel
*[Meditations on the
Christian faith and life]*

**Single Sentence
Sermons**
[Workbook for growing faith]

Lasting Love
[Short Biographical Sketches]

Walking in Faith
*[Much of the same poetry as
Faith and Yosemite but
without pictures]*

Living for Jesus
*[A Gospels Study Guide for
Couples and Small Groups]*

**Deliberately
Growing Spiritually**
*[A five-year Bible reading
program for spiritual
transformation.]*

**Spiritually Growing
Through Prayer**
*The focus is upon personal piety
and spiritual growth through
prayer.*

Christian Fiction

The Camera Doctors
*[Two people meet on top a
famous mountain, and
romance ensues.]*

An Extensive Life
*[The life story of a man who
lived more than
four hundred years.]*

Casting Lots
*[Christian romance and
adventure set in the near
future]*

**Empty Tomb,
Full Hearts**
*[A Selection of Testimonies
Among Those Who Saw
the Risen Christ]*

**Christian Romances
in the Foothills**
*An anthology of Tom's Town,
Soul Mates, &
The Camera Doctors*

The Gaardian Saga
*[Christian science fiction
fantasy with God in a major
role.]*

A Nation Transformed
[A future tale of God intervening in the USA with miracles.

Prayer Warriors
[Urban adventures in a near-future continuation of Casting Lots]

Soul Mates
[Romance, the same setting as Tom's Town]

This World Is Not My Home
[Two together since high school separate to find love with others.]

Tom's Town
[Small town life and Christian romance]

The Warrior and the Prophet
[God has surprises and blessings for newlyweds]

Yosemite Picture Books

Ever-Changing Yosemite Valley
[Yosemite Valley is a glacially carved valley. Moment by moment, scenes change.]

Faith and Yosemite Fourth Edition
[Pictures of Yosemite National Park, with poems about the Christian faith]

Portraits of El Capitan
[El Capitan rises 3000 feet above the floor of Yosemite Valley]

Portraits of Half Dome
[Half Dome marks the east end of Yosemite Valley]

A Sense of Wonder: Yosemite
[A Christian poem about Yosemite, illustrated with pictures]

Starlight Over Yosemite
[Large pictures of Yosemite taken at night]

Yosemite Textures and Shadows
[High definition photographs of Yosemite Valley, depicting all seasons, both day and night.]